THE LAST SERVER

H.J. PANG

With the support of

NATIONAL ARTS COUNCIL
SINGAPORE

© 2020 Marshall Cavendish International (Asia) Private Limited
Text © H.J. Pang

Published by Marshall Cavendish Editions
An imprint of Marshall Cavendish International

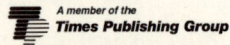

All rights reserved

No part of this publication may be reproduced, stored in a retrieval system or transmitted, in any form or by any means, electronic, mechanical, photocopying, recording or otherwise, without the prior permission of the copyright owner. Requests for permission should be addressed to the Publisher, Marshall Cavendish International (Asia) Private Limited, 1 New Industrial Road, Singapore 536196. Tel: (65) 6213 9300. E-mail: genref@sg.marshallcavendish.com
Website: www.marshallcavendish.com/genref

The publisher makes no representation or warranties with respect to the contents of this book, and specifically disclaims any implied warranties or merchantability or fitness for any particular purpose, and shall in no event be liable for any loss of profit or any other commercial damage, including but not limited to special, incidental, consequential, or other damages.

Other Marshall Cavendish Offices:
Marshall Cavendish Corporation, 99 White Plains Road, Tarrytown NY 10591-9001, USA • Marshall Cavendish International (Thailand) Co Ltd, 253 Asoke, 12th Flr, Sukhumvit 21 Road, Klongtoey Nua, Wattana, Bangkok 10110, Thailand • Marshall Cavendish (Malaysia) Sdn Bhd, Times Subang, Lot 46, Subang Hi-Tech Industrial Park, Batu Tiga, 40000 Shah Alam, Selangor Darul Ehsan, Malaysia.

Marshall Cavendish is a registered trademark of Times Publishing Limited

National Library Board, Singapore Cataloguing in Publication Data

Name(s): Pang, H. J.
Title: The last server / H. J. Pang.
Description: Singapore : Marshall Cavendish Editions, 2019.
Identifier(s): OCN 1121162583 | ISBN 978-981-48-6815-0 (paperback)
Subject(s): LCSH: Organized crime--Fiction. | Dystopias--Fiction. | Singapore--Fiction.
Classification: DDC S823--dc23

Printed in Singapore

This work was produced during the 2016 Mentor Access Project by the National Arts Council, Singapore.

To my characters, who insisted on their stories being told. One can only do so much to block out their voices.

To my Ma, who encouraged me to write, study and work at the same time. A juggling act of sorts, but then, everyone's an acrobat in their own way.

Come on, Greg. Get a move on already!

PROLOGUE

Greg clutched his right arm, wheezing hard with his back against the wall. Blood ran down its length, soaking into a battered elbow guard. The sounds of semiautomatic gunfire echoed from the other side of the room, their loud echoes bouncing off the electromagnetically shielded walls. Right across from him was a dead commando of the Old Guard, lifeless eyes staring accusingly back at Greg.

He knew the end was near. Who was he to believe that he could take on the might of an entire triad crew, with only the help of a computer cultist and an old commando? The 418 Dragons triad may not be as well trained, but they were far better equipped and prepared than a washed-up soldier like him.

Right in the centre of the room was humanity's last server, its superclocked processors humming serenely in the midst of shouts and gunfire. Before the control interface stood the computer cultist, Wesley, his body trembling as countless streams of data passed through his cerebral datalink. Even for a steadfast devotee of the Code, the security protocols of the server were fast taking its toll on his mind. Several figures lay upon makeshift beds set in a circle around the access point, maintaining their unconscious vigil. Wires trailed from their heads to the central control point.

"Get down, Wesley!" yelled Greg, yanking his last grenade out from a pouch. He fumbled with the pin, but without warning, the wall to the server room was blown in, showering him and Wesley with fragments.

Greg lay groaning on the cold, hard floor with a sharp ringing in his ears, praying that if he and Wesley were to die that day, all they had worked for would not be in vain.

The fate of the people rested on them both.

WHAT HAPPENED AFTER

Two and a half days ago

GREG'S GRANDFATHER ALWAYS said he never liked the Causeway. To him, it represented a precarious dependence on another. It was at this border crossing that billions of litres of water had flowed through pipes, the daily lifeblood of an island nation until it realised that having it home-made was so much less trouble. It was across this bridge that countless traffic jams occurred, every single day, where frustration and sheer boredom threatened to kill those in line. After all, the two countries' mobile data plans weren't interchangeable.

And here Greg now was, standing atop an old SBS bus overlooking its entirety. Up above shone the late morning December sun through a patch of clouds. Ahead of him, millions of dollars worth of COE lay rusting and abandoned, their value further depreciated by the long-looted engines and headlamps. Once something only the well-to-do could afford, these cars were now discarded like trash on the broken road. An old billboard six years out of date advertised the Singapore Airshow. Upon the horizon lay the hazy outline of what used to be home to Greg, but now all he could feel was a sense of trepidation as he surveyed the skyline, once filled with looming structures, now with hills of rubble. No city had ever looked more forlorn to him, not even the dilapidated facade of Johor Bahru. This was how things were in the world now, a world he had wished his children would not see. But it was far too late for that.

The way across the old Causeway was treacherous, and Greg was impressed that the structure still stood, six years after The Storm. Sections of bridge had been pulled apart in places, noodles of rusty rebar holding them together like precarious threads. Breaking into a run, Greg leapt across a gap, landing hard onto the hood of an early-model Toyota Avanza. He stiffened as the underside of the car groaned against the tarmac, shifting from its years-long rest. Greg scrambled quickly across its rusty surface as the vehicle pitched over the edge of the bridge, his feet landing on concrete just in time. He looked back at the car in its descent, which landed with a resounding splash in the murky water.

That was close. Even on water, a fall this high could kill. But a larger gap loomed ahead, with only the concrete dividers by the side still intact. Steeling himself, Greg held onto the railings, sidling his way across slowly but steadily. Twice, the concrete beneath his feet crumbled, and he had to quickly reaffirm his grip.

His arms and feet were already aching by the time he got to where the car inspection areas were. The cars were parked permanently at their eternal graves, no chance now of ever clearing customs. Their windows long since smashed in, not even the seats remained. Entire conduits of wires had been ripped out and pilfered for applications in the post-Storm economy.

"Eh! Who are you?" demanded a voice.

Greg turned quickly, dropping into a crouch. He had gotten careless. Three men emerged from behind the surrounding pillars and an old immigrations booth. All wore the signs of hostility and hard living: dust-coated skin and eyes that always seemed to glare. Unlike most wastelanders Greg had encountered, however, these guys lacked that hunger in their eyes. Yet the weapons they wielded betrayed their potential for trouble. He could handle the two parangs, but the scratched Taurus 85 police revolver posed a problem.

"It's okay! I'm not here for trouble!" Greg raised his hands and tried to back away towards the edge of the bridge, but the one with the revolver stepped towards him, weapon sights raised to his face.

"I asked who you are! You better answer!" he snapped. Despite being the smallest of the three, he carried himself confidently. Most likely the leader. He was the only one who wore the same grey jacket that Greg did.

"I'm a runner from the 418 Mines! I'm on your side!" Greg said. "Here, let me show you!" He drew the sleeve of his jacket up slowly, exposing the armband he wore beneath. A crudely-dyed image of a flame between a hammer and pickaxe showed itself, clinging tightly to a well-toned bicep.

The trio's leader looked towards his armband briefly. A look of mingled surprise, along with shock crossed his face as his men shuffled their feet.

"You're with the Minelords?"

Greg nodded.

"From whereabouts, exactly?"

"The mine of Teluk Ramunia! I've come bearing a message for this outpost. So if you'll let me …" He gestured to the satchel by his side.

The guard leader turned to a scruffy, bearded man with a scar across his left cheek. "Rashe, go get that from him. Shen Ren, cover Rashe. No funny moves, understand?"

"I'm Greg. Greg Lin," said Greg, forcing a smile. "I've also brought some treats for you all. Goreng pisang from a stopover point."

"Goreng pisang? Gimme lah!" snarled Rashe. He snatched the satchel from Greg, and turned it upside down. A short parang and half-full bottle followed by two sheets of folded paper and a bundle landed with a thump. While Shen Ren picked up the messages, Rashe tore apart the bundle's wrapping. He was already munching as Shen Ren handed the papers over to his leader. The leader read the folded messages as Greg waited.

At long last, he lowered his gun. "Good of you to bring these to us. I'm Liang. We haven't heard anything for a long while from the other 418 outfits. How long did you take to get here? Did someone drop you off?"

"A few hours," lied Greg. He followed as the leader beckoned them to follow him. Already the tension was dissipating. "A truckload of our enforcers were passing by, so I managed to catch a lift near to wherever they were going." The quieter of the two peons, Shen Ren, took a swig of water from Greg's bottle before passing the satchel back to him. "You're the 432 for this outpost?"

"49er in command," corrected Liang. The Minelords were under the umbrella of a larger triad called the 418 Dragons. After The Storm rendered much of the populace defenceless, the once-divided secret societies formed a union. By killing off all the other bosses, the current leader established himself as the Dragon Head, the highest position in a triad. No one knew what his real name was, but his vision had allowed for much of the surviving population in what was Southern Malaysia and Singapore to be enslaved for the triad's interests, one of which was tin and bauxite mining, which fell under the purview of the Minelords. And within a triad were separate subgangs called crews, or outfits. A 432 denoted the rank of "Straw Sandal", which was basically a liaison officer between the separate crews. A 49er may be a rank-and-file member, but senior 49ers like Liang were effectively crew supervisors. Although the triads of old traditionally conversed in various Chinese dialects, most had switched to English after The Storm. After all, there were non-Chinese gangsters and slaves as well.

They approached a cluster of shacks in the style of zinc-roofed attap houses, which had made a comeback after The Storm. It didn't take much except the simplest of materials and skill to put together. Smoke billowed from behind a shack, accompanied by the smell of rancid cooking.

"Well, Liang, one of the messages is meant for 418 HQ, so I'll need it back," said Greg, sneaking a glance at Rashe and Shen Ren. They were more engrossed in the pisang than the conversation. "I wouldn't want to forget to bring it to them."

"Eh, you new or what? All messages to HQ will be forwarded by us," Liang finally turned around. Up close, Greg could see a coldness in his eyes that his two raggedy men didn't have. "We will allow you to stay here at this checkpoint for no longer than the next morning. By then, a transport should arrive back at your designated pickup point for you to return back to Teluk Ramunia. And while you're here, you're not to stray from the checkpoint, understand? And we'll hold onto your parang for you. Here, you're already under our protection."

Greg contemplated this. He had to get to the 418 Dragons HQ at Fusionopolis, and that was a long way into the island.

But these guys were already wary of newcomers, and he wasn't going to get anywhere with their eyes on him.

"Go get something to eat from our cook," said Liang. "Rashe will show you around after you're done. Water rations will be handed out at 3pm today, and right before you leave tomorrow. Dismissed!" He stalked away while Shen Ren and Rashe accompanied Greg to a shack. Thick white smoke was billowing behind it.

If this was the way the 418 treated their own people, Greg had no doubt that he would fare much worse if they knew what he actually was. Slaves from the mines didn't have any rights.

Rich or poor, no one was spared when The Storm happened. No one truly understood what actually transpired. What was agreed on was that it had happened on a Saturday night in Singapore. One moment, life went on as normal. The next, entire power grids went out. Then came the fires, which started from the explosions of vehicles and fuel containers.

But that wasn't the least of it. Buildings collapsed into themselves, their rebar interiors twisting apart by strong magnetically-induced forces. Entire city centres and HDB estates crumbled, and many said this alone resulted in the loss of more than eighty percent of the population.

It wasn't only the destruction that awaited the survivors, but also the lack of information on what had happened. Any communication devices that weren't fried received no signal. With conventional methods of relaying news out for the count, mass panic ensued. No one knew if the country was at war or even if a natural disaster was responsible. Nobody knew if it was just Singapore, or if the same thing was going on in the rest of the world. Rumours about a solar storm or electromagnetic pulse attack ran abound, and no one was able to dispel such notions. On the plus side, there was no social media to give rise to more panic.

The Home Team and SAF were in disarray themselves. Having relied on radio and phone communications for years, their attempts at relaying orders by hand were further complicated by the burning heaps of vehicles in their possession. And the citizens themselves hadn't been idle. Some mobbed the governmental buildings, whether to complain or receive free aid. Others started looting stores and establishments, emboldened by the mass disorder. The more sensible ones tried to leave the country.

Greg still remembered the day it all happened. A day he wished would not replay itself over and over in his mind. He had awakened to the sound of crunching concrete, and managed to rouse his Lee Ping and the kids in time to evacuate their HDB building in Tampines. As they huddled at the car park along with their neighbours, it was clear that the four-storey building would not collapse completely. All it suffered were deep cracks throughout.

Greg's three-year-old Toyota Lancer, the one he had bought with years of savings, was now a burning wreck. A few vehicles stood intact, but they didn't have the keys in them. Greg could see the taller twelve-storey flats weren't as lucky as his building had been. Entire HDB blocks and high-rise buildings had collapsed, and it was only months later that he found out that unlike shorter buildings, the weight of the high-rises caused them to exert more weight on their cracked foundations, resulting in their ruin. The screams of crushed residents filled the neighbourhoods, and Greg had to keep urging his family to move. Several times they were almost robbed by looters, and Greg's military training had proved to be more than useful. By the tenth collapsed building, Greg realised they might have a better chance in neighbouring Malaysia. They had to head to the Woodlands Causeway.

It took them until the next night to reach there. It was far more crowded than he had ever seen it, far worse than the queues for the National Day Parades. Not so much with vehicles, as had generally been the case, but with throngs of people desperate to get across. Police and army personnel tried and failed to maintain order as members of the crowd attacked and pushed past each other. Then police vehicles were set on fire, the heat and smoke spurring the crowd to greater violence. Barricades, soldiers and police officers were pushed over and trampled. Greg knew he should be helping his fellow soldiers, but he had a wife and two kids to think about. Several times during the dash across the Causeway, he could hear gunshots. Twice he was almost separated from his kids in the surging mass of people, and he even had someone try to snatch his bag from him. That person had regretted it ever since.

Everyone had believed things were better on the other side of the Causeway. But they were soon proven wrong. Perhaps Greg's family would still be together, had they stayed where they were. And perhaps, he would not be on this quest to find his missing son.

The thing about The Storm, or the apocalypse, was that it came a long time after mankind believed technology would always exist. With so much depending on computers and electronic infrastructures that sustained the once-modern world, it was bound to happen sooner or later.

Like many of the settlements Greg had seen, this checkpoint wasn't so different, utility-wise. The nearby immigrations building was now a collection of ruins, but a camp had been built up around it. Construction canvas screens wrapped into cones fed morning dew to old plastic pails for drinking. Pieces of plywood and office partitioning formed the shacks. An open manhole topped by a chair with a hole made up the toilet, and Greg wondered what anyone would do should it ever get clogged. But all these were far better than the amenities back in the mines.

Though there were about six shacks here, Greg couldn't see or otherwise hear anyone else within them. He followed Rashe around the shack that was emitting the smoke.

Here, the smell hit him the hardest. With only walls on three sides, the building was laid out in the style of a kopitiam, reminiscent of a village-style eating place. Red plastic chairs stood around two tables made up of stacked concrete slabs. Old Tiger, Heineken and Carlsberg beer bottles decorated the sides, along with an old, tattered flag of the opposition party. Behind a long counter made up of two stacked benches was a kind of stove made up of concrete blocks. At the fire fuelled by scraps of wood, a bare-chested cook tossed some rice about a wok. On his back was emblazoned the head of a snarling Chinese dragon, ringed with skulls. Without counting, Greg knew there were eighteen of them. He'd been slogging in the mines long enough to count the skulls every member of the 418 Dragons had.

"Eh, uncle! We got visitor! Liang say you give him something to eat," blared Rashe. The cook turned around.

"He from where?" he asked. Greg could see that his tattoo was replicated on his chest. "Wah, you got pisang don't want share with me?"

"How I know you want? Here lah, here lah!" Rashe picked out a piece with a grubby hand, tossing it over to the cook. The cook snatched it deftly, popping it into his mouth. He crunched the snack with evident pleasure, eyebrows raised to Greg. With greying hair and a pockmarked face that always seemed to smile, the cook looked to be about fifty. Despite his evident gang affiliation, Greg couldn't quite picture him as a foot soldier.

"I'm a runner from Teluk Ramunia," confirmed Greg. "A raiding party gave me a lift to the other side of the Causeway."

"Must be hard to come here," said the cook. "I don't think now have enough bridge left to cross." Like many of the older people Greg had met, he spoke Singlish in the old style.

"Where got enough bridge," Greg replied. "A car almost took me along when it pitched forward."

The cook laughed, slapping his hands onto his rotund sides. "Wa kau. Someone's COE gone forever liao. But then, the gahment always tell people don't buy car."

Greg forced a smile, and the cook continued, "Really sibei jialat, but probably no longer his pasa. We haven't got runner come for very long time. You ride on truck so long then cross bridge, must be very tired. Here, you come eat." He held up his wok, scraping the rice out onto a large dried banana leave. "Uncle give you extra fish I catch yesterday." He plopped a small fish on top.

Rice wasn't all that common after The Storm. What little rice was available was now grown by slaves primarily in the fields of Selangor. And the slaves didn't get any of it. Although fish was plentiful in the rivers and sea, the fact that few remembered traditional fishing methods meant that gathering it was too much effort to feed a settlement of any size. An exodus of people travelling in search of food meant many were scattered far from their hometowns.

The ikan kuning and rice had the faint smell of unrefined palm oil, which was the cause of the rancid smell, but Greg wasn't going to turn down a free meal. He took the leaf bundle gratefully, and rolled the contents into a cone. He then proceeded to eat it Minelord-style, biting the rice wrap, leaf and all. As he chewed, his tongue found the leaf fragments and spat it out.

"So what's your name, and how long've you been a mine runner?" asked the cook. "You want you can call me Uncle Ong."

"I'm Greg Lin. It's been about three years."

"So what you do to prove yourself?"

If he wasn't that well-versed in triad traditions, Greg would have been taken aback. "I pursued an escaping slave and killed him. I had to track him through tough terrain. Very swampy."

"Wah, really shiong, sia," said Uncle Ong as he scratched his belly. "Very easy have foot rot like that. So how? You 49er now? Got family or not?" Greg's mouth opened, then closed. "No, I don't."

"Guy like you, how can not have? You go other mining town cannot find meh?" Uncle Ong laughed. "Not just lucky for you, also lucky for her. Your kind of looks very hard to find, confirm can get one. Uncle tell you, find someone higher, then you yourself can go higher easier."

Greg chewed his fish carefully. "As you say, Uncle," he replied. He looked around his surroundings. Rashe still sat at the corner, sifting through the stray pisang crumbs at the bottom of the packaging. He couldn't see the other two gangsters he had met earlier, so he took the chance to ask, "How often does anyone come down here? It's hard to believe you just grow and fish for your own food. Is it just the four of you here?"

"Of course not lah," said Uncle Ong. "There are actually ten people stationed here. Not including me, Uncle old liao but still can cook. Each outpost by the right have someone bring rice and other barang-barang every two weeks. But then here rarely got people want to go through Causeway, what more very hard to reach." Uncle Ong gestured towards the open side of the kopitiam. A wide expanse of broken highways and buildings went as far as the eye could see. A faint haze stood in the air, and somehow Greg knew it was the wind stirring dust from the old concrete.

"I mean, here got what?" continued Uncle Ong. "So end up we have to go collect our food and extra water ourselves. Bur what to do? Our Red Pole say do then must do lor. So six of our guys are now coming back from The Mountain with the makan and water."

"How do you know they're not still there?" Greg asked carefully. He figured The Mountain had to mean the 418 Headquarters, but confirming it would only lead to suspicion. Suspicion that could get him killed.

"Aiyoh, three days already! Go there only need two days mah," said Uncle Ong. Having reclined on one of those rubber-threaded deckchairs similar to what Greg had seen his grandfather use years back, the plump cook was now fanning himself with a plastic fan sporting a faded logo. "Hopefully this time they manage to get some Coca-Cola." He licked his lips.

Greg was glad the 418 didn't keep in contact with this outpost by radio. Few working electronic devices were available after The Storm, and certainly not two-way radios. The only electronics that had a chance of surviving the geomagnetic storms that made The Storm a reality were those that had been kept in metal containers. From the radio equipment he'd seen back at Teluk Ramunia, the 418 must have been resourceful enough to raid the police and military stores for it, and repurposed them for their own uses. Despite being secured by near-indestructible Abloy locks, an abandoned camp and police station could only hold out scavengers for so long.

"So how do the guys go to The Mountain? Do they walk across the Old City?" asked Greg.

"They have ways. That's all you need to know." Uncle Ong winked.

Greg didn't know it at first, but he had made his first mistake. After looking over his shoulder for last few days, getting the chance to relax had made him lower his guard. He should have noticed that Rashe, who was supposed to be watching him, was now at the entrance to the kopitiam with his leader and Shen Ren. The hostile glares they directed at him told him something was up. As he made to stand, the click of a revolver hammer reminded him of his place.

"You know, I just realised something strange," said Liang thoughtfully, the eyes behind his revolver glittering with malice. "You say you're delivering messages from the Ramunia mine. And yet, they didn't have the coloured logo of our brotherhood. Take off his jacket!"

"I'm one of yours!" protested Greg as Shen Ren came forward, his own parang raised. Uncle Ong looked worried, but didn't get up.

"Then you won't mind showing us the Tattoos of Loyalty!" yelled Shen Ren.

Greg slammed the sharper end of his spoon into Shen Ren's

neck as he neared. Shoving the spluttering Shen Ren forward as a shield, the 49er jerked as he took two shots from his boss before bowling Liang over. Rashe screeched as he leapt atop a table, swinging a plastic stool into Greg. The ex-soldier grunted as the sun-bleached plastic shattered, but otherwise remained standing. Knowing that it wouldn't be long before Liang got back up, Greg flattened his left hand, slamming it hard into Rashe's throat. The thug let out a strangled gasp just before hitting the floor.

Greg reached Liang just as the 49er pushed the motionless Shen Ren off him. He fired off a deafening shot as Greg dodged, and the two of them scrabbled for the gun. Greg knew that ammo was scarce, so he slammed Liang's hand hard against the uneven concrete. The gun fell with a clatter, and Greg then set about demolishing the crew leader with his fists. Rage from years of being locked up in those foul mines exploded out of him, and soon all that was left of Liang's face was a dark, crimson mess.

Greg sat astride his victim for a while, panting. He took hold of the revolver, and checked on Rashe. He now lay with his head at an unusual angle. No way had he survived that. Greg was about to search the place for anything of value when he heard panting from the back of the kopitiam. Raising the sights of his revolver before him, Greg rounded the corner.

Uncle Ong was sprawled against a mess of broken wood, one of the piles that had fed the cooking fire. He was clutching his leg as he grimaced, and by the look of the swelling on his ankle, it had gotten twisted during his escape. His eyes opened wide as Greg came closer, the worn revolver posing an unspoken question.

"Don't shoot Uncle Ong! Uncle Ong never fight you …"

whimpered the old gangster.

"How do I get to Fusionopolis?" demanded Greg. "What?" Uncle Ong's face looked confused.

"Don't pretend you don't know!" The toe of Greg's boot slammed into Ong's ankle, causing him to yell. "Where is the HQ of the 418 Dragons? You want me to shoot, is it?"

"You mean The Mountain?" gasped Uncle Ong. "Only Liang and the others know the route. I old liao, never go there before …"

"I can always shoot you and find the way there myself," shouted Greg. He didn't have much time; if what Ong had said earlier was true, he had only maybe an hour to search the place before the rest of Liang's crew turned up. Even with fully-loaded gun and parang, it would be presumptuous to assume he could take on a group of seven and live. "Does Liang have any maps? Where the hell are his quarters?"

"No maps." Uncle Ong slowed his breathing, wincing as he moved his leg slightly. "There's no easy way to walk across the country. The guys have their own route through the old HDB estates. But then … look, Uncle also don't want you to die. There are raider patrols all across the island, and the old HDB places sibei dangerous."

"I'm touched. Is there another way there?" demanded Greg. "I don't think my finger can hold on any longer."

"W-w-wait! Got another way!" Uncle Ong's eyes flickered. "Nearby here got an MRT station. I think called Woodlands Checkpoint. It leads underground to the Brown Line. From there you can make your way to your Fusionopolis."

It looked like there was no escaping the use of the MRT even after The Storm. The rapid transit network of Singapore's public transportation system was mostly underground, and could have bypassed much of the topside's destruction. A number of these stations were designated bomb shelters, after all.

"Why don't the guys use it?" Greg asked. A trap, perhaps. All these criminal types were well known for that.

"A lot of barang-barang block the way … the guys need to bring stuff through …" wheezed Uncle Ong. "Also, they scared got things down there …" The old triad member looked up. "Look, I already say what you ask. I even warn you the place damn dangerous. I go now, can or not?"

Greg lowered his gun. He remembered his family being taken from him. He remembered his wife being beaten and killed as her murderers laughed. He remembered his children being taken away, never to be seen again.

He really hated the triad responsible for that. Greg raised his gun and fired.

Greg would normally have cleaned up after himself, but here there wasn't any point. Even if he removed the corpses, there was way too much blood for him to clean off, and the disappearances of the remaining guards would raise suspicion anyway. There wasn't much of value in the shacks—it was obvious that even among their own triad, nobody trusted each other enough to leave their valuables behind. Greg found a Swiss army knife and several water bottles, taking care to fill them up at the water points he had seen earlier. He also got hold of a small, china-made alarm clock that had somehow escaped the ravages of The Storm and a roll of nylon rope he recognised as SAF-issued tenting line. He was down to his last round of ammunition for his revolver, and Liang didn't seem to have any more. However, the 49er had one of those angle-headed flashlights the army used to issue, that appeared to be powered by home-made batteries made of electrical tape, washers and salt water. The triad members also carried at least two pieces of gold and silver each, along with some differently-coloured leaves of paper. Greg peered closer and saw the insignia of the 418 Dragons at the top, followed by a serial number. This had to be their in-gang currency. A search of the shack that Liang kept locked yielded a poster with the 36 Oaths handwritten in English, a fresh set of clothes, and some dried strips of meat, but no ammunition or even an empty speedloader. Guns must either be in really short supply, or reserved for the best 418 fighters. Greg knew he didn't have long to leave, but something Uncle Ong said bugged him.

There had to be a reason why the guys didn't use the MRT tunnels. Perhaps there were parts that were structurally unsound, and all that was needed was a careless scavenger to loosen enough of the rubble. There would be loose wires and faulty electrical components along the stretch of the track, but Greg doubted there would be any electricity left after all these years. But he was in unknown territory, and he wouldn't last long out in the open. Skulking in the tunnels would be the best option for now, and he could always get out at any station along the way. Greg recalled what he remembered about the route, and walked into the old immigrations building.

The MRT network of Singapore was so ingrained in Singapore infrastructure that many of its exits led straight into public buildings like malls and hospitals. During the planning of new train routes, a member of parliament had proposed that an MRT station leading directly to the basement of the immigrations building would ease the daily jam faced by the vehicles queuing across the causeway. He couldn't have been more wrong. The ease for day-trippers heading into Malaysia had resulted in a threefold increase of visitors to the checkpoint, and getting one's passports stamped had taken longer than before. Incidents of people illegally walking across the Causeway multiplied, and the MRT station then known as Woodlands Checkpoint soon became something of a joke.

Large gaps that had sprung in the immigrations building allowed Greg to enter. He found himself in what was once a vast hallway, now criss-crossed with crumbling sections of wall and columns. Being a short building, it hadn't fully collapsed under its own weight. Halfway across the hallway were the faded immigration booths and automated gates, with a ray of sunlight illuminating them. Several skeletons littered the floor, their mouths open in silent screams; one was sitting against the wall, his bony fingers raised in the grasp of a phone long-since stolen. A section of metal ceiling covered him below the waist. He was probably trying to tweet about it—#apocalypse #ohgodwhy #woodlands #rockandhardplace—when The Storm happened. The silence was reminiscent of a graveyard. And in many ways, Greg thought, he was in one. Reaching the booths, Greg saw that anything of value, including the fingerprint and passport scanners, had long been stolen. Two Immigrations and Checkpoint Authority officers could be found among a few other civilians near a broken side door—probably died trying to herd them out of the building. Greg found two biometric passports and a couple of pens on the ill-fated travellers, and pocketed them. He could do with something to write on. And perhaps one day, the passport's ID page could be placed in a memorial to those who had passed on.

Greg had never alighted at this MRT station, but he was able to follow the dusty signs that led towards it. The LED display signs that used to show train departure times lay over the escalators leading into the station. Greg half-expected the signs to indicate that the train service in all lines were currently disrupted, and to expect ten more hours of travelling time, but The Storm had done its job well. With most of the metal steps and steel sheeting gone, exposing the broken screws and sharp edges within, Greg treaded his way carefully down into the station entrance. The shutter doors that had once kept out intruders had been wedged open by a concrete slab, with a couple of gouges suggesting where others had pried it open. Peering cautiously into the unlit tunnel, Greg crawled into the belly of the beast.

The mines were a harsh, unforgiving place. It was a place where people worked, lived and died. It wasn't like they had any other choice. All who worked there were slaves.

Greg had been slaving away for five years by then. In the first week after The Storm, he and his family travelled far enough to find a village to stop in. There wasn't much to be done, but the local police sergeant understood the value of a man like Greg. Along with a few other able-bodied refugees, he was given a job as a militiaman, while his family helped out at the palm oil plantation and farms. The Storm did not seem to have altered any natural life in the slightest, and life still went on in the farming towns. About half of the palm fields were razed and turned to farming food crops for the village. Several times, the village saw soldiers of the Malaysian army pass through on bullock carts, stopping long enough to load them with food and other supplies. No one had ever thought they would see the old modes of travel make a comeback, but almost all motor vehicles were toast after The Storm.

The first few months after The Storm were chaotic. Refugees and soldiers alike could be seen passing the roads, including members of the Singapore Army. There were always wounded to see to, and those who didn't seem to have any useful skills were turned away whenever they tried to settle. More times than he could count, Greg and the other militiamen had to intervene when bands of looters raided the village—he still had the scars to show for that. He had since learnt to keep his parang close. Eventually, even the soldiers stopped passing through.

One year was a very long time. Long enough for the organised gangs to build and equip their standing armies. Long enough for them to start looking for greener pastures. And Greg's village was in their way.

There was nothing a twenty-man militia could do against a war party of two hundred. And parangs and hunting rifles were no match to armaments that would put any police department to shame. The village of Shumai was razed and pillaged, and those who weren't killed in the raid were led away in ropes and chains. Greg knew then the fight was lost. He would have fled, but he had a family to take care of. They would wait for their chance to escape.

That chance was lost when they were led into the mines of Teluk Ramunia. Deep in the tunnels, the only way out was death. Greg was the only one known to escape alive.

BENEATH THE NATION

Nobody liked using the MRT system. With its overcrowding, constant breakdowns, and the repetitive announcements via PA system, it served only to remind commuters what they were missing above ground. Greg had thought he was done with all that after The Storm, but some things always came back to haunt him. He threw the beam of his torch around. The glare of the light reflected back by the plastic-lined wall almost blinded him. Somewhere in the distance, there was the sound of dripping water. Walking down the dim entranceways, old billboards long out of date still remained on the walls. One of them showcased happy children holding packets of some obscure brand of juice Greg hadn't had the foresight to try. Now he never would. Some of them had been smashed in by scavengers looking for fuses and light fittings. A picture of an unpopular local artiste had been scrawled on, though he wasn't sure whether it had been vandalised before or after The Storm.

But then, some things never changed. Four ticketing machines, previously faced with impatient queues of people, now stood forlornly at the far wall, unused and unwanted. The glitter of coins and one-way tickets lined the floor before them, useless now. Made of plated steel, the newer coins weren't even worth the price of scrap. Making his way past the smashed-in control booth, Greg stepped his way carefully down the escalator leading to the train platforms, his boots giving out a clunk every step of the way.

A rustle to the left side of the platform caused him to turn quickly, the beam of his light flickering across the glass of the doors. Probably rats. Greg stepped over to a map of the train network and peered at it, wiping off the dust with a gloved hand.

He knew he couldn't completely trust what Uncle Ong had said after his cover was blown, but he didn't doubt that the 418 HQ was at Fusionopolis. After all, he'd heard it straight from the most reliable of sources. All that remained was how he was going to get there.

Greg was now on the Thomson-East Coast Line, so he could walk along the stations and transfer to the Circle Line at Caldecott, and take the route to one-north station, which lay directly under Fusionopolis. This was barring any cave-ins along the way, of course. From his own experience, nothing ever went according to plan. Alternatively, he could transfer one station away at Woodlands station, then go along the North East Line to Jurong East Interchange ... no, that wouldn't work. The majority of that line was above-ground, and likely to have crumbled since The Storm. And anyway, it defeated the purpose of him trying to travel underground in the first place. The topside could be far more dangerous than he knew, and he wouldn't accomplish his quest if he were to be hit by random sniper fire. A pointless end to a most difficult task.

And so that left only one route. Hopefully, he would be there before day's end. "You want go where, sia?"

Greg almost jumped out of his skin, but his clothes must

have kept it in place. The weak beam of his flashlight jerked erratically as he fumbled in search of the voice's source. A dark-skinned figure sat with his back against a nearby pillar. Because of the debris obscuring the guy, Greg hadn't noticed him. Despite being covered with dust and grime like everyone else he had met, the speaker was dressed in what looked like a tattered red shirt and black pants, and Greg would be damned if that wasn't the old uniform of an SMRT service officer, complete with name tag. Next to the guy was a couple of empty snack packets and plastic bottles.

"Who the hell are you?" demanded Greg, composing himself quickly, gripping hard on his unsheathed parang. Twice he had been caught with his guard down, and the hard thumps of his heart reminded him not to do that again. Damn, that guy could have had a knife in his back in that time he took to examine the map. "And what are you doing here?"

The guy frowned, shading his eyes from the beam. "Can don't shine light. Very bright leh …"

Greg reached out his free hand and lifted the man by his front, slamming him against the wall. The bang echoed across the whole station, and the beam of the light shone nearer into the vagrant's eyes. He wriggled weakly, but it was of little use. He was much lighter than Greg had expected; malnutrition was a far too common problem in the wasteland.

"I ask a fucking question, you give a fucking answer!" yelled Greg. He was past caring if there was anyone else nearby. "Are you 418? Tell me now!"

The man blinked several times. Wondering if the guy was a retard, or just plain stalling, Greg turned and flung him hard across the platform, where he skidded upon the shards of concrete. Greg stepped after him with his parang raised.

"418? No, but the people upstairs are," said the man, pointing upwards with a confused expression. "Why you don't like 418? Ya, I know they laugh at me, but they also give me food and water. Sometimes even a bit of nasi lemak." He got up, brushing his shirt out with his hands.

"My name Muthu. I MRT station manager."

"Don't be stupid. The MRT system was destroyed six years ago, along with everything else," growled Greg. "Stop wasting my time, dumbshit. Why are you here?"

"MRT not dead. Just asleep. Waiting for the time to wake up," sang Muthu. "So I wait here for passengers, make sure they wait behind the yellow line. Move in, bags downs, shuffle to the door! And when they're done …"

Unbelievable. The world after The Storm was a brutal place. And yet, retards still found a way to survive after all that. Ignoring the Bag Down Benny ditty Muthu was now singing, Greg found a piece of rebar and pried one of the platform doors open. He lowered himself slowly onto the tracks, where darkness and musty air enveloped him. The chattering of the imbecile followed after, a haunting tune that raised the hair on his arms.

The tunnels of the mines were dark. And from the very minute the prisoners from the war party's raid had arrived, the pecking order of the mine's hierarchy was established.

The mine foreman, a man Greg remembered only as Towkay, had walked before the snivelling prisoners, twirling a revolver in his hands. Stripped down to the waist, his tattoos extended all the way to his eyes. Holding his pants up was a chain that clinked with every step.

"I am called Towkay, and this whole place is my house!" Towkay had announced. He needed no loudspeaker. "And in my house, we have rules! Rule number one is we don't allow weakness!" And right before everyone, he shot a skinny prisoner in front of him. Everyone jerked back, and tried scrambling away, only to be shoved back by the guards.

"Rule number two, you work or die!" This time, he fired at another victim, a limping man. Greg had fought to stay calm as his children and wife cried. He couldn't tell them to be quiet, or Towkay might turn his attention to him.

"And rule number three, you listen to us!" Towkay finished his speech by pointing the gun at the group. "Does anyone else need to be shot?"

Everybody had then been forced into different lines. Whatever remained of their old selves were confiscated, including their clothes. Greg later saw one of the guards wearing his shirt and jeans. They were issued a random assortment of shoes, smock, pants and belt. They rarely fitted, and Greg was lucky enough to swap his with another man. An unwitting prisoner tried to tell the issuing guard his shoes didn't fit, only to be smashed with the butt of a rifle. They were herded deep into the tunnels of the mine, where the darkness swallowed them. None of them, except a rare few, ever saw daylight again.

The ramblings of the lunatic followed Greg for some time as he walked through the gloomy tunnels, and he counted himself lucky that no one was around to hear it. The last thing he needed were a couple of rogues tracking him down. After The Storm, no one hesitated to kill for even a gulp of water.

Walking towards the dark hole that was the MRT tunnel fringed with the fading light from his torch, he could hear the occasional clanks and thuds from far away, and already he could feel a quiet eeriness creeping over him. An old MRT wreck stood in his way ahead, its emergency door open on the tracks. This was one of the newer automated trains. Climbing through the exit, it was all he could do to walk through the passageway of metal and glass, the narrow expanse of space pressing against him. The terror of the mine's confines came back to him, and Greg tried to look forward.

Remarkably, much of the train tunnels and trains were still in almost pre-Storm condition. Being underground must have helped, with the electromagnetic fields having passed through the surface structures instead. The MRT stations would thus have made good homes for people, if it weren't for the fact that the triads would sooner enslave people than live up to their purported principles. But these trains were practically bare of any human habitation. Sure, there weren't any belongings around, but that could always have been a result of looting. The raised gate Greg himself entered from said that much. He plodded on through the train, and fell back onto the tracks. The other stations along this line were otherwise insignificant, and he passed them by without incident. He would have stopped to raid the stations for anything of use, but he had to make good time while it was still daylight. By the time he got to Caldecott, Greg could feel the long-familiar pull on his stomach. He checked the clock he had taken. It was now 3:26pm. He hadn't eaten since before dawn, when he managed to steal the goreng pisang from a 418 checkpoint. Just a few more stations, then he'll stop for a bite. He had to make these rations last till tomorrow, at least. Greg knew he had to reach Fusionopolis before day's end.

Otherwise, the discovery of his handiwork at the checkpoint would potentially alert 418 HQ, making it harder to get into.

The newer interchange stations on the Circle and Thomson-East Coast Lines had cavernous hallways between the transiting lines, and Caldecott was no exception. Greg had likened them to the underground military bunker he had been in just eight years back while inspecting stored ammo. Here, the chaos of The Storm was more apparent. Someone had driven a van through the escalator entrance of an MRT station, crashing it through the hallway. The van now lay forlornly in the hallway, a bare skeleton at the wheel. Short of being a last-ditch attempt to get into the station, the burned-out headlights and interior suggested the van was one of the few on the road when the geomagnetic storm occurred. The driver must have careened off the road as his electronic control system failed, only to find his vehicle crashing through the entrance to the underground MRT station. Long since collapsed by a mix of factors, the debris of the station entrance barely let in any light and air, and Greg started sweltering from the heat. With The Storm taking place in the wee hours of the morning, there weren't supposed to be any passengers in the train lines. But the numerous discarded food and drink containers suggested that it had been used as a shelter at some point. Greg entered the control room with its dusty charts and controls, and found a bunch of keys. They probably only worked for this station, but some of them had to be master-keyed, meaning they would work on multiple doors. He found the direction of the track that would lead towards one-north station and walked through the dim hallways, back to the platforms that would take him to his destination.

Greg remembered a time not so long ago. It had been December, two months before The Storm. Lee Ping had wanted to take the kids to a toy fair at Suntec City. With the weekend ERP, and so little parking lots, he'd decided not to drive. Jin and Mei made a big hoo-ha over not wanting to stand during the train journey. But that was how so many people got to work and school each day, and Greg wanted to teach them the lesson that not everyone was fortunate enough to have a car to be driven in.

Strangely enough, the two kids enjoyed it. The twins had looked in amazement at the giant fans at Tampines station and noticed how much cleaner and shinier things looked on the Circle Line. Mei especially liked the glittering metal sculptures at Promenade station. She declared that she wanted to be an artist some day. The automated train system on the Circle Line had made Jin talk all day about wanting to be a programmer.

Greg stopped in his tracks. Jin.

Jin was the only last shred of his family that remained. The twins were due to start primary school a month later. Greg could still remember one of the questions Jin had asked him two days after the toy fair.

"Pa, will I learn how computers work in school?" Unlike most kids, he didn't play any of the Android or Apple application games. Rather, he always explored the source code in the settings, and once reformatted his mother's phone by accident. Were it not for Greg, she would have killed him.

"It's not just in school that you learn things, son," Greg had told him, as he worked through several army technical manuals on small arms. "Every time you seek to find out more, you're always learning new things. It is only through never stopping that you truly understand how everything in the world works."

"Okay, Pa. Can I read whatever you're reading?"

"You can't. Only army personnel are allowed to."

"Aww."

"When you join the army one day, then perhaps I'll let you read them."

Jin and Mei had started school, only to have it cut short. On 15 February, The Storm happened. Some called it The Switchoff, on account of the near-total loss of electronic technology. Yet others called it The Second Fall of Singapore, referencing the very same day Singapore fell during World War II. But to Greg, it had resulted in the loss of his own world. His family. His home. All because the bloody triads saw fit to oppress everyone, using their violence and guns and damned ideology as an excuse for it. And now he had to make this damned journey, just because some triad admin couldn't leave his family the hell alone, just to do some sick shit Greg knew nothing about.

Greg yelled in frustration, kicking at the steel-framed glass door to the platform. The double-layered glass cracked slightly, but otherwise held, and the web of cracks across Greg's reflection only served to infuriate him. He roared, delivering a spinning back kick to the glass, and only then did it shatter, the clatter of glass resounding across the platform.

A howl came in the distance, and Greg stumbled, almost falling over in shock. The echo lingered across the vast expenses of the station as his eyes darted left and right. What the hell was that?

He cursed, peering carefully out from the gap in the platform. All he could see was the darkness of the tunnel ahead. A rumble came from ahead, followed by the sound of shuffling. Greg waited for a while, and it was only when his neck ached before he advanced, parang out before him. Something told him he should turn back, and get away from this madness, but the alternative held no appeal for him. There was no way out at Caldecott, and who's to say he wouldn't get shot at once he was out in the open? At the very least, he could deal with any wild animals with his parang. He was starting to wish he hadn't wasted a bullet on Uncle Ong, but for all his affableness, that guy deserved to die like the rest of the triad scum. Creeping forward in the dark tunnel, Greg turned off his torch. He crept closer and closer to the next station, praying that he would not find what he thought the sound was from.

For a long time since the MRT network was built and repeatedly expanded upon, people believed that certain stretches of the MRT were haunted. Stories were abound about ghostly sightings in the dead of night, and they mostly centred around the stations which had been built on former gravesites. But there were also stories about ghostly sightings elsewhere, and phantom trains appearing at ungodly hours. Even in the 21st century, belief in the paranormal was a staple of Singaporean culture. There was even a whole book series on it, along with several knockoffs. Greg himself had read the books when he was a kid, and considered much of it creative fabrication. But no retelling of paranormal tales, no matter how gruesomely told, could have prepared Greg for this.

Right behind the glass doors to Botanical Gardens station, Greg could see several figures crawling on all fours, snuffling and letting out growls. Around them were piles of what looked like fruit peels, leaves and parts of trees. Interspersed among the plant matter, however, were the unmistakable shape of bones. A femur could be mistaken for a stick, but there was no mistaking the characteristic prongs of a human ribcage, and the three gaping holes of a skull. The stench emitting from the station of rotting fruit, flesh and excrement assailed Greg, but what truly got his attention were those figures shuffling about the platform.

They were people, but no longer people, if it came down to it. They were unmistakably human, still donning the rags of their former clothes. But their skin was of an unwashed pallor, with nails that had grown long and encrusted in the grime of the past few years. But it was their faces—taut muscles contorted in constant snarl, with eyes dilated beyond recognition—that showed they had lost all trace of their former selves. One of them bumped into another, and the other snarled, the two of them tumbling in a whirling, spitting mass of fury. Several of them gathered around and hissed, not unlike a pack of beasts.

Greg felt sick. He didn't know what these creatures were, but surely his nightmare couldn't get any worse. Feral humans were something one saw only in the movies of old, not in real life. He scrabbled towards the direction of the next station, and stumbled, pushing himself back up with his hands. His feet scrabbled against the gravel of the sleepers, and that was when the problem started.

One of the ferals turned quickly at the sound, spitting and hissing. Padding towards the glass door of the station, he slammed his hands up against the glass doors of the station, his gaze locking into Greg's. Dressed in the tatters of a transit security guard's uniform, the feral's skin was covered with filth. Two jaws of cracked, yellow teeth showed as he snarled, breath misting the glass.

The moment he lifted his head and howled, Greg knew he had no time to lose. Even as he ran, the tinkle of glass rang at different points throughout the platform as the ferals slammed themselves against the glass, hands scrabbling through holes and cracks. Their snarls and cries chilled Greg to the bone, and part of him hoped that he would awake only to find that he had dozed off at a station, and that this was all one bloody dream. But the burning of his legs felt real enough, along with the rancid stink emitting from the station.

Noticing the wiring conduits at the side, Greg drew out his roll of tenting line, as he maintained his pace, looping it quickly through the mass of wires from one end to the other. Leaving the X- barricade behind him, Greg ran on, the sound of metal and glass landing onto tracks and gravel following close behind. Caterwauls and shrieks followed soon after.

He knew his trap had worked when he heard the distant sounds of gagging and snarls, followed by the scattering of gravel. Some of them sounded like they had started to fight against one another. But the ferals wouldn't stop for long, and Greg still had four stations to go, if the MRT map was anything to go by. Despite years of hard labour in the mines, Greg hadn't had much opportunity to exercise his legs. When food was scarce, and sleep the only respite, one didn't waste it on needless movement. This much was apparent as he felt the muscles of his leg burn, his breaths coming in hard and fast. He was desperate to stop for a breath, and maybe a drink of water, but any second spent stopping meant an extra ten or so metres closing between him and his pursuers.

As Greg passed Farrer Road station, a figure pounced from the platform, and Greg had just time enough to duck as the figure caught him across the top of his back, sending him tumbling into a roll. As he turned, the newcomer clawed at Greg, and it was all he could do to hold his assailant back by the neck. This feral looked thinner and more underfed than the ones in close pursuit, but was still strong enough to not allow Greg any room for movement. Greg yelled as the feral snapped close to his face, its bad breath stinking up his nose. Arching his back, he used his momentum to fling his attacker over, sending him crashing into the edge of the platform.

By the time he managed to get to his feet, Greg found himself surrounded by a few of the ferals from the previous station. He lifted his parang slowly, keeping his eyes trained on them. Already, he could hear the transit security feral making short work of the one that had just attacked Greg, its snarls and gurgles dying off into silence. It appeared that these ... creatures had some sort of territorial nature. Only the strong survived. How ironic that he had survived five years in the mines, only to be killed by monsters straight out of a movie! Greg could barely see the silhouettes circling him, so he turned on his flashlight.

The feral right in front of him hissed, standing upright as her hands shielded her eyes from the glare. Another to his left pounced, and Greg swung his parang hard, catching him on the skull. Another charged from behind, and Greg turned too late to intercept him. The loud bang of gunfire rang out, and Greg saw his attackers fall away in a splash of blood. A nearby feral sank his or her teeth into his jacketed shoulder, but Greg felt the weight slump off him as another shot found his mark. Towards the next station, several flashlights on the track turned on.

"You there! Come to us!" barked a voice. In the confines of the tunnels, no one needed a loudspeaker. Greg lifted his hand to shield his eyes from the glare. "Stand there for what? Hurry and run lah!"

Greg needed no telling twice. He stumbled towards the direction of the voice and light, doing his best to shield his eyes. The next few shots echoing through the tunnels hurt his ears, but he was well aware of the splats of flesh and bone behind him. When Greg finally reached the source of the lights, a strong pair of arms lifted him up onto the floor of some kind of railcar. He was shoved onto a bench, and as his eyes adjusted, he could see the guys who had saved him. One was standing against the railing at the railcar's front, firing away with a SAR 21A rifle. With their flash suppressors, barely any muzzle flash illuminated the surrounding area. The railing itself had two construction lights mounted upon it, throwing strong beams towards the front. Greg could see the ferals caught in the wide beams as they scarpered or fell from gunfire. The shooter's partner pushed repeatedly on a lever set in the centre of the railcar, and it quickly reversed with the constant sound of rubbing metal. The railcar was manually operated! With the rarity of improvised fuels, Greg wasn't too surprised.

The rifleman wiped his brow and turned to Greg. "What were you thinking?" he snapped. "You should know better than to walk these tunnels."

Now that he wasn't running for his life, Greg took a good look at his saviours. The one heaving away at the lever wore an old-style Load Bearing Vest, or LBV, over a singlet. Greg could see the hints of tattoos peeking out of his collar, and across his forearms. Another SAR 21A was likewise slung across his back. His partner seemed to be better equipped, with a pair of night-vision goggles strapped to his head. He had raised it up before turning on the lights. Around his bicep was the red armband of the 418. Greg was about to jump off the railcar, but the look from the 418 shooter wasn't exactly hostile. He then remembered his guise still remained.

"What were those things?" croaked Greg. The lever operator found a bottle of water and passed it to him. "It's ... it's almost like they were ..."

"Zombies? No, they not undead," said the rifleman as he reloaded his gun. "More like gong-gong already. You heard about the auroras that formed after The Storm? The people who weren't indoors at the time went siao after seeing it. The lucky ones just become a bit crazy. The not-so-lucky ones?" The rifleman jerked his head towards the direction they'd come. "Lots of these siaokia were created. We call them the Mindless. I heard people say it had something to do with the cosmic radiation frying their minds or something, but I also don't know too much about it. They usually stay underground during daytime, with their eyes being light- sensitive and all, so we try to keep away from the underground stations."

"But there're ... there're so many of them," said Greg.

"Well, the Botanical Gardens station is one of the most infested. Some of the brothers say that a number of the animals that escaped from the zoo settled there, because of all the fruit trees in the area. The Mindless also like fruits, but love meat more." The rifleman peered at Greg. "You from which outfit?"

"The Minelords," said Greg, flashing his own armband. "I'm one of the messengers for Teluk Ramunia."

"So how come Liang never forward the messages?" asked the rifleman. Greg could see that his eyes were narrowed. "He normally will do that, what."

"He must forward, meh? It's an urgent delivery to a Red Pole, so he say I must hurry up go!" Greg banged on the bench. "But that bugger never tell me the MRT is dangerous, almost get me killed! Now I also want to tell his Red Pole what he did!"

"Eh, relak, okay?" said the rifleman quickly. "Everyone makes mistakes lah. Liang should tell you which route to use, but he couldn't have known you would use the MRT network to get here.

It might be a lot faster if we didn't have Mindless crawling about, and if there weren't, we would already have expanded into all these stations. Lim and I will bring you to The Mountain to deliver the message alright? Then we'll see about getting you back to the Causeway. I'm Yin, Senior 49er."

"Greg, 49er messenger," said Greg, shaking his and Lim's hand. "The equipment you all use really stylo-mylo."

Yin laughed. "Eh, 418 treat their best people well, you know. Besides, we also need this stuff. Anything else won't be as effective in these tunnels. You think MP5 got use here? Range too short. What more, 9mm ammo not as powerful." He smacked the pistol at his waist regretfully.

"What are you guys doing here anyway?" Greg asked. "It's quite far from The Mountain."

"We have an outpost at Buona Vista station," clarified Lim. "We heard some noises, including what sounded like an actual person, so we went to investigate. You're lucky we found you when we did."

"Ya, but also very fun for us," said Yin, smacking his rifle. "This gun damn fun to use, and what more, can do full-auto some more. The Mindless don't dare came near Buona Vista, because of the lights, but they also know we've got guns. They may be siao liao, but they aren't 100% stupid."

They were silent for a minute as they passed Holland Village station. Several figures flitted away into the shadows, and Greg had no doubt they were stray Mindless, if not other forms of wildlife. Yin kept at the lookout, but despite the railcar moving at a relatively slow 20 km/hr, nothing came after them. They soon reached Buona Vista station. Several oil drums with fires burning within lit the area, along with two high-powered overhead lights focused towards the front. Three guards and their weapons were silhouetted against the light.

"Hey, Yin, what you find?" yelled one of the figures as they neared. Greg could see him manning a fourth-generation FN MAG machine gun mounted on its tripod, complete with targeting system and its long belt of golden rounds.

"A fellow 49er lost his way! I'm going to bring him to The Mountain!" replied Yin. Greg could feel the eyes of the guards boring into him. "Shouldn't take more than thirty minutes."

"Let him walk himself, lah!" said one of the guys. "Not like very far what."

"Kani nah, is that how you treat your brothers?" questioned Yin. "Next time you on forward duty, you can go yourself!"

Greg briefly wondered how long it would take for them to realise he wasn't who he said he was. He had to remain silent. Making a move now would only result in him being cut down by that MG, and a half dozen rifles. He took several breaths to calm his nerves, even going as far as to rub his hands together. Lim looked curiously at him.

"This your first time here?" asked Yin. They had come up to the station platform. The glass of the doors had been reinforced with wooden boards and sheet metal. Just beyond it, another guard post could be seen. "Don't need to worry, our guys won't anyhow tekan you one. Just relak, and let me do the talking, okay? After you deliver your message, I can take you to makan and maybe drink something. Our cookhouse makes very good teh and kopi." As they neared the metal-framed glass doors of the one-north station platform, he reached out his hand and rapped the doors several times. A guard at the post nodded, and picked up a nearby handset. He spoke a few words into it, and to Greg's surprise, only the doors they were at opened. The 418 had really thought it out from a tactical standpoint. In the event that the forward outposts got swarmed, any adversaries would have to enter a single door, putting them at greater risk of being gunned down. The lights at the station were lit in alternate rows, and Greg couldn't remember the last time he had seen real artificial lighting. The mines had single bulbs at some places, but their glow was so intermittent that it always had to be supplemented by candles. Rolls of makeshift barbed wire directed traffic towards the escalators at both sides of the platform.

Greg followed Yin and Lim up the closest flight of escalators. As they walked past the control room, one of the three guards stepped out towards them, and the group stopped. Here, only a single light lit the immediate area.

"Who's this?" asked the guard. Having grown his hair long unlike the other 418 members, it fitted around his head like a lion's mane. Upon his vest were the English numerals 426, identifying him as a Red Pole, a senior commander of a triad crew, who may be tasked with special duties such as assassination. Bare arms lay at the side of his ballistic vest, and Greg could see the landscape of tattoos upon it. Now that he stood up close, Greg could see that they were names. Written in both English and Chinese script, Greg guessed they may have been the names of his victims.

"Messenger from The Minelords, Red Pole Keng!" affirmed Yin with a salute, clenched fist over his rifle. "I was just bringing him upstairs."

Red Pole Keng looked Greg in the eye. "And why didn't you give the message to Liang?" he hissed.

"The dispatch was urgent, Red Pole, and it was important that it reached its recipient," replied Greg. "There's been a complication at the mines."

"A complication like … a mine escape?" asked Keng.

CAPITAL CITY OF THE 418

"That's right," said Greg. He didn't know how Keng knew. He'd made sure the communications equipment at the mines were completely and utterly destroyed. But he was going to have to improvise as he went, otherwise he was totally screwed. He stole a look behind him. Behind, several walkways to the old mall above stood. All of them had fire gates raised, but he was still fifteen metres away, at the very least. "I'm bringing the dispatch to the Incense Master…" He took two steps backwards.

Yin raised his eyebrow. "Just now you said you're supposed to give it to a Red Pole." Greg cursed himself.

Keng whipped out his pistol, with the two guards in the booth following suit. The sound of cocked slides and hammers echoed throughout the station. Yin and Lim stood undecided as Keng stepped towards Greg, his face livid.

"So you're a stinking 25, eh? A fucking spy?" roared Keng, as Greg kept his hands raised. "Do you know what we do with spies?"

"I'm no spy!" exclaimed Greg. Already he could gauge he was about ten metres away from the door. But he would be cut down the second he tried to run.

"Show me your tattoos! Show me your fucking tattoos!" screamed Keng, froth flecking his mouth. "Take off that jacket and show me!"

Greg gripped the bottom of his jacket and pulled. As he flipped it over his head, he spun, drawing the revolver he hid in his waistband. Aligning it with his target, he fired.

The single lit bulb shattered, throwing the station into darkness. As one, the triad guards opened fire, lighting the area sporadically. Stepping to the side, Greg flung his jacket towards Keng, and the Red Pole yelled, spinning around wildly. Two of his shots were accompanied by yells, but Greg couldn't see who it was. He ran through the open fire door, and struck the button next to it. The fire door came down with a crash, and almost immediately, the indents of the bullets striking the other side appeared on the surface, followed by rifle rounds which pierced through it completely. With no time to waste, Greg ran up the escalators to the upper floors. He was out in what was once Nexus mall. Out here, what little daylight that remained was filtered in through the glass above. Two guards raised their rifles at the sight of him.

"There's a 25 downstairs!" Greg yelled. "The Red Pole needs your help!" Eyes wide open, the guards ran down the escalator, leaving Greg to slink through the guard post, but not before grabbing what appeared to be a floor plan. He quickly headed towards where he saw a line of people, following close behind. None of them looked back, and Greg could see from their haggard and grubby faces that they were exhausted. With more males than females, in their hands were what looked like gardening and digging equipment, including spades with dirt on them. It had to be about 6pm now, the time the work crews typically knocked off.

Looking around, Greg could see that what remained of the old shops were now occupied by stalls. All seemed to be utilitarian in their offerings, selling stuff like food and drink, which likely included the kopi Yin had promised. There didn't seem to be any other offerings such as clothes. Looking ahead of the line he was following, Greg saw that they were depositing their tools at a counter, where two similarly haggard workers yanked it from them, an armed 49er in a red armband watching them. An older man wearing goggles sharpened a tool against a rotating block of concrete, looking briefly at Greg. The group walked towards the old escalators to the upper floors, with Greg close behind. And just then, an alarm sounded. Greg couldn't believe it, but the sound appeared to be coming from the old fire alarm system. The 418 had managed to repurpose it for their own uses. Several guards dashed past with an assortment of weapons. It wouldn't be long before the guards were out looking for him, but he had to blend in for now.

The upper floors of Nexus had wide open spaces. Once meant to appeal to mall-goers, it was now cluttered with numerous tents mixed with structures of cardboard and plywood. The glow of flames could just be made out reflecting against the structures. Here, the work crew dispersed, some heading into what passed for home, while others made their way towards the wall at the far side. The sound of running water could be heard nearby, and Greg headed towards it.

A single hose fed several taps which some of the grubby workers washed themselves with. Several plywood booths had been set up side by side over a channel that acted as a drain for who knows how long, with lumps of mold growing in it. One of the booths opened slightly, and Greg could briefly see someone scooping some water from a basin with a cup, and dousing himself with its contents. Just like how his grandfather had showered back in the old kampungs. Still, this was far better conditions than many other places Greg could think of. Stepping inside an empty booth, Greg drew his utility knife, quickly shaving off thick clumps of his hair and beard. He followed an approximation of a style that most of the men around here had—short and unkempt. Not having any means to dry off, Greg settled for washing just his face and arms. He changed into the fresh set of clothes he had taken from Liang before heading out.

There was some sort of commotion going on, but Greg hadn't heard it during his trim. His stomach chilled as he saw several 418 soldiers taking up positions around the living quarters, kicking and pushing tents down as they did. A pot propped over a fire toppled, precious stew sloshing over the floor. Several villagers were grabbed and yelled at, with a couple ordered to place their palms against the wall. Greg saw several of the nearby villagers kneeling with their hands behind their head, and quickly followed suit.

"Has anyone seen anyone that doesn't belong here?" yelled a soldier. One could tell by the better equipment he carried, along with the red words painted on his clothes, that this was a Red Pole. Nobody answered.

"You!" Greg's heart jumped as the Red Pole stepped towards him, flanked by two 49ers. "Tell me if you've seen anything!" He was grabbed by the front of his shirt, and pulled upright. Up close, the Red Pole's breath smelled strongly of marijuana, probably consumed right before his raid. One of his enforcers swung his baton, and Greg jerked as it made contact. A sharp pain seared across his skull.

"I didn't see anything," spluttered Greg, fighting to stay

conscious. He was glad he'd left his bag in the shower booth. A quick search by the enforcers would have blown his cover. For now, shaving himself put him in the part of a lowly worker well enough. Part of him was wondering why no one squealed on him, but he was otherwise occupied with the guy holding him.

"Liar! Surely you had?" yelled the Red Pole. This time, a punch crashed against Greg's stomach, doubling him over. He gasped, tensing himself to ready the Swiss army knife he had. He wouldn't have a match against the other armed enforcers, but at least he wouldn't go down without a fight.

"None of us saw anything, Red Pole," said a voice. The Red Pole whipped around, and Greg fell to the ground. He was vaguely aware of the enforcers moving away from him, but pain prevented him from doing more than tilt his head up.

It was the guy with the goggles Greg had seen earlier. Now with his goggles hanging around his neck, he was speaking calmly to the senior triad member, despite being a head shorter than he was. Dressed in work overalls, he had a couple of tools on his belt, which was surprising, given that Greg had seen the other workers returning them. Back in the mines, slaves didn't get to bring their tools back to their quarters, for fear of a revolt or sabotage.

"Everyone here knows the importance of security, Red Pole Wan," said Goggles. "I didn't see anybody that I didn't recognise at my post downstairs."

"What would you know? You have your eyes on your tools all the time!" snapped the Red Pole.

But his tone was less hostile than before.

"As Blue Lantern, I am just a commoner helping the 418 and not a sworn member, but I am also in charge of my brothers' security," said Goggles. "And I know the 418 rewards those loyal to the cause. Many of us here aspire to be part of the brotherhood someday, and would never jeopardise that. You have my word that we'll detain anyone who looks suspicious, and let the enforcers know about it. I swear it."

"Swear by the Oaths," yelled the Red Pole. "The whole damn lot of you."

"We swear by the 36 Oaths!" everyone chorused. Greg didn't manage to catch that in time, but the triad members were no longer looking at him. Red Pole Wan gave a snort, and brushed past Goggles.

"If you see anything suspicious, report it!" yelled the Red Pole to all who were gathered. "The first one who does it gets promoted to 49er, along with 2000 Dragon dollars!" With a clomp of boots, the triad enforcers left.

"Get back to your business, everyone!" Goggles called to the crowd. "Let's get everything back in order, or we're going to have our meals late." He went over to Greg. "Come on, back to your feet."

Greg allowed himself to be pulled back up, averting his gaze. As he made to move away, Goggles followed close behind.

"We have to talk." The tone wasn't threatening, but it wasn't one that took no for an answer.

"I'll be okay, Blue Lantern. Red Pole Wan didn't hit me too hard. I've got to attend to my duties now anyway."

"If you don't come with me right now, I'm going to blow your cover," hissed Goggles, and his tone made Greg turn towards him. "These guys might not betray you right now, but give it enough time and they would. If you risk the safety of my commune, I'll make sure you never make it out alive."

Greg clenched a fist. "What do you want?" he demanded. He retrieved his pack from inside the shower booth. He knew

Goggles hadn't saved him out of the goodness of his heart. There wasn't much community spirit to be had even before The Storm, and needless to say, nobody ever did anything for free these days. It was always something for something, for who knew if someone you met today would be gone tomorrow?

Goggles nodded approvingly. "Straight and to the point. But not in front of the others. For now, follow me. And put this on." He passed Greg a pair of welding goggles and a scarf. "If anyone asks, you're my workshop assistant."

Goggles went to his shack and found a stack of metal parts, and passed some of it to Greg. He then walked towards the exit of the commune, his new assistant in tow. There was a bare-chested 49er guard smoking a cigarette outside, armed with nothing more than a revolver and machete. This was unlike the well-equipped guards he had seen earlier, who had rifles and other mil-spec equipment. Goggles rounded the corner to where another door stood. Greg briefly saw a hand-drawn roster with two names on it before Goggles opened it, clanging it shut after him.

"Put that crap on the workbench over there," said Goggles before locking the door with a key. Greg dumped the stuff on the table, taking a look around.

Like many facilities in the post-Storm landscape, almost everything here was makeshift. Several shelves which looked like they had belonged to a shoe store were lined with metal parts of all shapes and sizes. On closer look, it appeared to be parts of machinery, including that for a building's ventilation system. Larger components, boxes and sheet metal were stacked against the wall. On the wall was an English translation of the 36 Oaths, which looked to be handwritten on a panel that made up a false ceiling. The workbench itself wasn't an actual workbench per se, but an office desk with several metal clamps bolted onto it. An open FM radio lay on its side, with its screws and a side panel removed. To Greg's amazement, a DC power supply was attached to the mains supply, with boxes of wires and scavenged electrical components next to it.

"You have electricity here?" There was little need for him to deny he wasn't from these parts.

"Only for the Production Centres and some workshops," said Goggles, settling into the stool at his workbench. He gestured towards a box that Greg could sit on. "But that's only from 6am to 6pm, so we have to get anything done electrically between then. Only the restricted areas, or those with special requests, get light 24/7."

"Production Centres with electrical infrastructure? That's better than I expected."

Goggles snorted. "I'll love to talk about the wonders of The Mountain, but I'm sure you haven't come here as a refugee. So how about we get straight to the point?"

And so it begins. "You said we need to talk. So what do you have to say for yourself?" demanded Greg.

Goggles took off his scarf and his namesake goggles. "I saw you when you were following the guys returning their tools to the collection point earlier , but didn't tell any of the 418 about it. It didn't take long, however, before the 418 sent their raids. Your very presence almost brought disaster upon my commune. With close to twenty communes just like the one you were in, it's not uncommon for the 418 to purge one as a warning to the others. As a responsible leader, I should be turning you in, if only to protect my own people.

"That said," added Goggles as Greg got up in fury, "you're the first guy to have broken through the 418's defences in a year. The last one lasted no more than five minutes, and he was a member of the Old Guard. If anything, their guys have some of the best fighters in what's left of the world. Given your achievements, I believe we can do business."

"With whom do I have the pleasure of working?" sneered Greg. "And why should I be working with a 418?"

"Because you know we have something to offer each other," said Goggles. "You have skills in deception and the ways of war, and I know every inch of these buildings. My name is of no concern to you, but you may call me Lantern."

"Fine, what do you want, Lantern?" snapped Greg. He remained on his feet.

"How about you tell me what brought you here first?" challenged Lantern, standing up slowly. "After all, I did save you from the Red Pole and his thugs." Up close, Greg could see his eyes carried a glint which betrayed the courage that came under hard conditions. This was a man who had worked under the 418 for who knew how long, with the threat of punishment and death for any mistakes he or his guys may have made. His eyes were also those of someone who put the safety of his own guys before anyone else, who wouldn't let a bigger and stronger thug bulldoze his way out of here.

Greg wavered, memories of long past flooding in. "I'm trying to find Jin." He slumped back to his seat.

Lantern tilted his head, eyes creased into a frown. "I'm afraid I don't quite follow."

"I'm trying to find my son. He'd been taken here," choked Greg. "I need to get him back."

Lantern let out a breath. "And what makes you think he even passed through this place? Maybe you should start from the beginning."

Each day at the mines brought only pain, and a growing sense of desperation that permeated the air like smoke.

The first few days were some of the worse Greg had known. Most of the slaves, fearing the fate of the gun or machete, had gone like sheep to their tasks. Three days had been enough to send a few others gibbering towards their captors, picks and shovels raised in defiance. The rebellion was over before it began.

A new batch of slaves had come in just the day before, so Towkay had seen fit to make an example out of some of them. Twenty more slaves were executed, with the entire slave population to bear witness. Since then, no one had dared try to revolt.

Greg couldn't be sure how many slaves there actually were. With the confusing mess of tunnels, one could count five on work detail on an ore deposit, only to see them again when they transferred the raw ore to the trucks that led to the surface. And one didn't exactly have the time or energy to count. If it looked like you were daydreaming, you got struck by a guard.

There was no way of telling time in the mines; only a lucky few saw daylight on the occasions they pushed the ore-laden trucks to the surface. Greg wasn't one of them. But a clock he had glimpsed in a guard post on the way to and back from his shift suggested work detail lasted from 5.30am to 7pm, including meals and breaks. Perhaps considered a flight risk, he was put on an excavation work detail deep in the mines. Like many of the women, his wife was tasked to food preparation duties, alongside the transportation of stores and water. The children weren't spared, either, and assisted the women.

It was three years later that Lee Ping was assaulted by a Red Pole. Like a true wife of a soldier, she fought for her dignity. But a half-starved woman was no match to a seasoned and desperate fighter. Despite it happening in the crowded food preparation area, no one dared do anything. Greg had heard from one of the female slaves that his daughter Mei had tried to help. She was beaten along with Lee Ping and taken away. Greg couldn't have done anything even if he had been there; it had happened in a different sector during work duty. He later heard that Mei had died from a concussion, and Lee Ping was given an off-the-books execution for resisting. Greg wanted revenge, anything to show that not all of them were sheep. But he still had his last kid to think about.

Jin always asked when they were going back to the kampung. Each time, Greg could only tell him it wasn't time yet, and convince him they were just here for a little while more. Eventually, Jin stopped asking.

When Jin was taken from him in the dead of night, at the age of 12, Greg knew his time in the mines was over. He had to find his son.

Lantern lit a cigarette. "I think I know where your son may be," he said.

Greg stood up and quickly wiped his face on a sleeve. "Where?" he whispered.

"Before you set about doing anything, you have to understand the situation here," said Lantern, holding his hands up. "So how about you sit down and listen to me first?" His face was impassive.

Lantern blew out a cloud of smoke, not bothering to face away from Greg. It gave off an acrid, bitter smoke, and smelled nothing like the pre-Storm stuff. "Where were you originally from?" he asked. "I'm guessing you were a slave."

Greg didn't see how it would hurt to tell him. "The mines of Teluk Ramunia." Lantern raised an eyebrow. "It's under the purview of the 418 Minelords in East Johor."

"I had heard of the mines that feed the war effort," mused Lantern. "But I've never been there. Me, I've been here ever since the world went to shit. Yeah, hard to believe, right?" He chuckled as Greg stared. "I was a maintenance technician for the A*STAR labs here at Fusionopolis and I had figured that with most of the survivors running across the Causeway, there would be plenty of work for guys like me. I wasn't entirely wrong; some of the more dedicated scientists were close to breakthroughs in research and wanted to see it through. Did you know that of all the buildings in Singapore, it is Fusionopolis that best survived? Some of the scientists say the large amounts of electromagnetic waves the machines here give off counteracted the effects of The Storm. It's all IT experimentation here, so any number of wireless signals could have caused it. Even the nearby buildings of Biopolis weren't completely spared.

"Anyway, it didn't take long for some of the criminally inclined survivors to band together and see this building as ripe pickings," Lantern continued. "They eventually became a big part of the 418 as we now know it. Their Dragon Head—that's the 418 chief— saw the importance of using the technology here to rebuild the future. Much of the computer data was corrupted during The Storm, and he needed people to work on recovering what they could. Many of the scientists and researchers came under their service. Those who were deemed useless …" He shrugged.

"Will you get to the point already?"

"Tsk, I'm coming to that. So anyway, the 418 knows all these equipment needs maintaining. A few of the technicians, including yours truly, are in charge of all that. Not just machinery, but ventilation, floor and electrical repairs. That means I have access to everywhere in the building. This includes the labs."

Greg sat up straighter.

"The labs are split between Fusionopolis and what's left of Biopolis," said Lantern. "Aside from those dedicated to IT operation, there are also small-scale assembly lines on the first and second floors. Scavenger crews bring back anything in the city that could be put to use. Now, I have seen kids in the assembly lines. Some of them are from my own commune, and I'll recognise any of them.

"But only a day ago, I saw a few unfamiliar faces in one of the labs. They had been locked in cages."

"Cages?" whispered Greg.

"That's right," affirmed Lantern. "One of the other maintenance guys confirmed he saw them wired up to some measuring equipment in the IT lab. The funny thing is that it's normally the guys in Biotech that handles living subjects. Now, one of these kids could be yours. I can take you there."

"What's in it for you?" asked Greg. This was the moment of truth. The price one had to pay for a service rendered. Somehow, Greg didn't think it would be any of the currency they used in these parts. But he couldn't give up on his son, not when he had a fresh lead.

Lantern stubbed out his cigarette on the edge of his workbench. For a long while, he said nothing. When he spoke, Greg could see a certain glee in his eyes.

"I want your gun," said Lantern. "I know you have one in your waistband."

"What do you want it for?" asked Greg, although he already knew. There was only one reason why someone would want a gun rather than a knife. It kills easily and quickly. Weak men became powerful fighters the moment they wielded them. It was the reason why guns changed warfare since they were invented.

Lantern's answer surprised him. "I want to make arms for my commune," he said. "When the time comes, the 418 will get what they deserve. We will take over the labs, and make sure no one suffers under the triads anymore."

"You'll be slaughtered. These aren't handgun-wielding lunatics you're talking about," said Greg. "This is a fully-equipped army, complete with rifles and GPMGs. I've seen them. Even in the off-chance that your makeshift weapons work, your guys are going to be outgunned. It'll be a bloodbath that would have no hope of succeeding. I'm not going to put anyone else at risk."

"That's not your concern. And that's my price."

Greg huffed. "Can't you smuggle out some rifles from the armskote or something? You did say that you have access to anywhere."

"If one of the 49ers at the armskote so much as discover a single magazine out of place, they're going to perform a building-wide search," explained Lantern. "Two years back, one of the knives in a cookhouse went missing. The 418 raided all the communes just to find it. And despite the fact that they didn't, the Incense Master had ten guys executed, and they weren't even on cookhouse detail. So believe me when I tell you that I'd already thought that over. I won't be able to help you unless you give me what I want. That's a promise."

Greg didn't know when he would get another gun, if ever. The wasteland was a very dangerous place, and there were few things more valuable than a working gun.

"Fine," Greg finally said, "but you'll get it only when we reach the lab."

"Deal," said Lantern. He got up, consulting a clock on the wall. "We should go after midnight. That's when there're the least guards about. I suggest you get some sleep. It must have been a long journey for you to come here."

"Nothing I can't handle," replied Greg. Weakness was never respected in the wasteland.

"I'll get you some stew. Best you don't show your face at the communal fire. The guys are a close-knit group, and we don't know who'll sell you out for a dragon dollar. It doesn't sound like much, but it'll get you half a full meal. You can sleep here till the time comes." Lantern pulled a section of plywood down to the floor. From the smell, Greg could tell it had been used for the very same purpose many times before. "If you need a piss, there's a bucket in the corner."

Lantern left through the door, locking it behind him.

Greg knew it was dangerous trusting anyone, especially someone who would love to get his hands on stuff he had no other way of getting hold of. But it had been a long day, a day filled with crazed victims of The Storm, murderous triads, and a nutcase who thought he was still the station manager of a long abandoned MRT station. A minute after he finished a stew he knew not the ingredients of, Greg was fast asleep.

The evidence pointed to Fusionopolis. Home of the 418 Triad. The hub of their war machine. That Greg had gleaned as he listened in to conversations among the guards. It was said that where industry had fallen throughout the known world, it was making a comeback in The Mountain, Capital City of the Southeast. It was considered both an honour and privilege to be even a slave there.

By holding a guard at bladepoint with a shiv he fabricated out of a sharp flake of granite, Greg found out what had happened to the missing kids, and he escaped within that very hour.

Most of the 418 members went bare-chested, with their tattoos paraded for all to see. It was thus impossible for Greg to impersonate anyone, but not so difficult to kill his way out.

The guards didn't expect a fully-trained soldier to revolt. They certainly didn't expect any of the slaves to get hold of a gun. But Greg did, and he lost no time in making full use of it. Starting off with silent kills, he had no choice but to resort to going loud near the entrance, where the most guards were. Having run out of ammo, and not wanting an entire fighting force pursuing him, Greg cut down the supporting timbers to the mine's entrance. Greg hated to see the last vestiges of working technology go to waste, but the radio station on the topside had to go. The wires and electronics were quickly reduced to an unsalvageable mess. No one would be using it anytime soon.

And without looking back, Greg knew his victory was bittersweet. Some would say he was now free. But no one is ever truly free until he is reunited with loved ones lost.

The metal door creaked open and Greg sprung up, parang in hand. He didn't relax even as he saw it was Lantern.

"It's time to go," said Lantern. He was dressed in the same clothes as before. Greg was wondering why he didn't change, but then, he would blend in wearing maintenance overalls should anyone challenge him. Slinging his pack across his shoulder, Greg followed Lantern out. He wondered if he should ask Lantern for a set of his overalls as a disguise, but Lantern would want deniability should things go bad. Greg didn't blame him; he might have done the same thing in his place.

Some of the lights were still on, but no one was around. Below the balcony, on ground level, two 49ers could be seen sitting on chairs. Nobody could be seen on any of the corridors, but Greg kept low anyway, taking care to look around corners before he proceeded. Blinking the sleep out of his eyes, he made sure his revolver was still secure in his waistband.

The complex had completely changed in character. Earlier in the day, there was always some form of activity going on, such as patrolling guards, or even commoners lugging their loads. But now, no such activity could be seen. Greg supposed that any guards still awake had their own manner of getting around. An R&D complex which housed several high-tech companies, research organisations, and government agencies before The Storm, Fusionopolis was a confusing mass of corridors, and if it weren't for his guide, Greg would have been hopelessly lost.

As they progressed forward, it was obvious that the way ahead was given to more high-tech facilities. Right before they rounded a corner, Lantern raised a hand to stop Greg.

"There's a security post right around here," he whispered. "It's manned at every hour of the day. The 418 doesn't want anyone sabotaging the research that's taking place."

Greg took a look. Up ahead, a series of window grilles that were salvaged from HDB flats were bolted together to form a kind of fencing. A set of double-gates were locked with a rubber-wound bicycle chain. Two more guards sat beyond. It was hard to tell if they were asleep through the grille at this distance, but it was obvious they weren't getting in this way.

"So what now?" Greg asked.

"There's a ventilation shaft we can use to get to the area," Lantern replied. "Follow me." Moving away a few metres down the corridor, Lantern opened a door. The smell of grease and dried sweat hit Greg. Rags and other unused stores littered the room, and he stopped rubbing his nose fast enough to see Lantern pulling off the cover to a shaft. Lantern pulled himself into it, and Greg followed suit. He would have liked to pull the cover back on themselves, but there wasn't enough room to turn around even if he wished to. He followed Lantern who had flicked on his lighter up ahead, the metal walls pressing in on him. As his eyes adjusted to the gloom, he could see patches of rust on the stainless steel walls. Some parts of the shaft looked like it had warped inwards, the uneven surface a consequence of The Storm, but Lantern simply crawled through those areas. Greg almost panicked as he felt his broader shoulders seized by the narrowed space, but a hard wriggle got him through. He made a right turn, then a left.

From his own estimate, they were past the checkpoint, and already a distance ahead of it. Lantern crawled over a hatch, and popped it loose after taking a look through it. The metal landed with a clatter and Greg froze, but Lantern slid through without pause. Following the handyman, Greg saw that he was in a janitor's closet. Rolls of cleaning cloth lined the shelves, with bottles of chemicals next to them. Two mops lay against the wall, with a pail of dirty water next to them.

"Do as I do," whispered Lantern, picking up a toolbox. He creaked open the door to the room, and Greg followed.

It was like stepping into another world. Where the drabness and destruction of the world was apparent even in the open spaces of Nexus, right before him was undamaged glass, metal and plastic. Clean corridors of polished tile stretched on, lit by fluorescent bulbs throughout its length. The contents of each individual lab were visible through the glass windows that framed their boundary walls. There was equipment he remembered seeing from his university and polytechnic days: measurement equipment such as oscilloscopes, thermocouples and multimeters, and testing rigs with clamps and prefab circuit boards. There were even working LED and CRT monitors with readings, attached to a mess of wires linked to racks upon racks of what could have been a LAN system. Despite half of the lights of the corridor remaining on, there was no one to be seen. So much undestroyed technology, and all of it right here, under the control of the 418. Greg could barely get his head around it all. One could awaken in these corridors and not know the destruction of the world outside.

"This is the lab they're keeping the kids in," Lantern pointed at a section they were walking towards. Here, the glass windows were lined with reflective film, so no one could see what's inside. "The cages are behind the mainframe computer that's been set up here. I'm getting the gun before I open the door." Lantern stopped before the door, holding out his hand.

"How do I know there're really cages behind there?" demanded Greg. "I can't have you making away with your prize while I go inside."

"Then you'll never know," said Lantern coolly. He turned

and walked towards the exit.

Greg grabbed him on the shoulder, but Lantern was ready. He swung his toolbox towards Greg, who barely managed to block it. Fighting back the dull throbbing spreading across his forearms, Greg twisted Lantern's offending arm, sending the toolbox clattering. Tools and fasteners of all shapes and sizes scattered across the tile. With his free hand, Greg grabbed Lantern around the throat. Pushing forward, he slammed him against the glass window of the lab.

"I'll get in, with or without you," hissed Greg. "It seems that someone thinks he's indispensable. All this for a piece of metal?"

A groan of a child could be heard and Greg froze, his fingers posed around his victim's throat. It came exactly where Lantern said it would. Greg backed off as Lantern made several choking noises, fumbling for the keys to the lab. He eventually got it open, and Greg dashed inside.

"What about our deal?" demanded Lantern.

"You'll have it when I come back out. That means you're going nowhere," Greg replied. He pushed past the equipment placed upon trolleys, and rounded what appeared to be an enormous computer setup. Another door led to a separate room, and Greg crashed inside.

The first things he saw were the cages spread across inside the entirety of the room. Hanging over them were wires and connectors of every conceivable type, and Greg could swear he could see connectors for Apple and Samsung devices. The cages were all empty, save one at the far corner. Walking slowly towards it, with his heart in his mouth, Greg got closer.

A boy sat hunched against the corner of the cage, clutching his head. He couldn't have been more than ten, and bore the marks of countless signs of abuse. Bruises, welts, even what looked like two-pronged marks that could have come from an electronic control weapon.

This wasn't Jin. The kid's shaved head had a number of probes attached. Two wires from the ceiling led to two of them, with the indicator LEDs glowing green. Shackles on his legs and arms kept them from removing the wires above.

Greg puked right on the floor. He had travelled far and wide, only to find that not only was his son gone, he probably had all manner of chips and wiring and whatnot installed into him, all as part of a sick experiment for who knew what. Only now did he notice that what he thought was rust was actually blood on the bars of the cages. Now that he was still, he could smell the piss and shit over his own puke.

"Who are you?" asked the kid. Greg stumbled back up, not even wiping his mouth on a sleeve.

He flattened his back against the bars of the cage behind him for support.

"I'm Greg," he said. "I'm looking for my son." He fought back another bout of nausea.

"There were other kids here," the kid grimaced as he spoke. Perhaps it hurt him just to speak. "A few of them stopped moving, and they took them away. But there were some who were still awake when the bad people took them."

"What about Jin?" whispered Greg. The kid looked blankly back. "Who?"

"Jin. My son." Greg gripped the bars. He backed away as the kid recoiled. "Look, kid, do you have a name?" he asked. He knew this was just a child, but he couldn't help but feel impatient. He had to get going, but something about the kid made him remember his life before.

"Oh, names." The kid thought for a moment. "Sorry, it's hard to think sometimes." He shook his head slightly. "I'm Guo Li. I only came in yesterday. There were four others here. The guys with tattoos get angry when any of us talk or cry, so I only talk to them when there's nobody around. I asked the others what their names were, but they don't remember much. The one next to me said he was called 1-1-0-7, and the one across is 1-1-0-9, but I don't think that's their real names."

Greg saw a medical clipboard affixed to the kid's cage and grabbed it. Scheduled Neuroimplanted Datalinkage and Cerebral Uplink Overhaul followed by a list of chemicals and readings—Greg didn't have to be a doctor or computer professional to know all this were bad news. The 418 had been tinkering with the brains of their subjects, sticking wires and who-knows-what into their minds. And with side effects, it would seem. According to the notes at the bottom, so far, no surgery or installation of any foreign devices had yet been done on subject 1108, who had been scheduled daily doses of some drug Greg couldn't pronounce. The short-term memory of the kid suggested some form of mind-altering drugs. Who knew when they intended to begin surgery. Tomorrow? After he had been deemed sufficiently sedated?

"What's this about?" asked someone to his right. Greg cursed his carelessness and turned. A guy in a lab coat stood at a nearby door. He wore goggles that seemed to increase the size of his eyes by five times and had hair that was scraggly, yet fluffed out. All this would have been incredulous if it weren't for the nature of this place.

"Someone who wants to know where his son is," said Greg, stepping forward with his revolver raised. "Believe me, with all the shit your people put me through, I wouldn't be surprised if

I shot you right now. Where have you taken him?" he screamed.

The geek barely flinched at this outburst. "Consider yourself a victim if you may, but many of us are no more free than these children were. It is only through conformance that we live yet."

"Where. The. Fuck. Is. My. Son?" bellowed Greg, and the geek found himself slammed across the cage. The kid squealed, but Greg was past caring about courtesies. He could feel the veins in the geek's neck budge, but didn't care.

"The thugs sent a couple of kids to the Last Server," choked the geek. "There, their minds will be put to the test in the digital and mundane. We know not what, save the Red Pole of the Labs."

This guy had the cheek to talk rubbish to him. Greg wouldn't have thought twice about breaking his neck, even in front of a kid, but once again, he had forgotten the most important rule of survival: to always be aware of one's surroundings. Only then did he realise they weren't the only ones in the lab.

"Put our guy down, you cheebai," said someone from behind. Looking back, Greg saw that the doorway he had entered was now crowded with 418 guards. All were decked out in full combat gear, complete with MP5 submachine guns and scowls. Right at the back was an angry Lantern. Even if Greg had a full cylinder of ammo to call his own, he would come out worse in a fight. He wondered if he should have given Lantern his payment, but there really hadn't been anything to stop him from turning on him either way.

"Take the glasses out of my coat pocket and put it on," hissed a voice, and it took Greg a moment to understand it was the geek who had spoken. "When the lights go out, follow my lead."

"What? I'm supposed to trust you now?" snapped Greg.

"It's your only hope of getting out alive," the geek replied. Greg saw how true that was. Already the 418 response team was creeping closer, and the only reason they hadn't opened fire was his close proximity to two of their assets—their test subject and scientist, if you could call the geek that. That could soon change.

"Whatever you're going to do, do it now," said Greg, his heart beating furiously as he slid a pair of oversized eyeglasses out of the coat pocket and over his eyes. "This gun of mine isn't going to do shit."

"As you say," replied the geek, as he reached for another pocket. Greg tensed.

"Why you take so long? Let him go!" yelled the 418 guard.

A number of things happened then. The lights went out, throwing the whole place into darkness. On reflex, Greg sprung backwards and dropped to a crouch. Gunfire erupted throughout the lab. Almost immediately, Greg saw to his surprise that the view before him was illuminated in a field of dark green, punctuated by bright strobes of SMG fire. The geek was dashing through the door he had entered from, and the illuminated display before Greg pointed an arrow towards him, complete with distance and destination. Night vision goggles coupled with real-time locator? Wicked shit. He ran through the door after the geek, keeping low as another staccato of shots erupted around him.

"Use your flashlights lah, fucking bodohs! Never use brain is it?" yelled one of the guards. Greg caught sight of the geek flitting into a room, and followed him closely. The geek slammed the door after him, wedging it shut with a table. Rows of bullet holes sprouting through the wood suggested how short-term this measure was.

"What do we do now?" yelled Greg. Around him were stacks of computer parts, along with unused monitors and CPUs. The lack of any other door suggested that this was a storeroom, rather than an actual part of the labs. The heads-up display on his glasses highlighted the geek in a reticule, accompanied by what he could only presume to be his handle, "ITm4ster". ITm4ster was now bent over the floor panelling, his fingers reaching under it.

"Help me pull this off!" snapped ITm4ster, and Greg felt around the edge of a floor panel. One of the door hinges gave in from a kick, but the table kept it closed. With a pop of plastic, the panel slid off, revealing cables and metal struts. Quicker than Greg would have imagined, ITm4ster dove headfirst into the gap, squirming under the hole's edge.

"Follow me and cover the hole!" came his muffled voice, and Greg did as he said. There was no space to squat, so it was an awkward position he found himself as he lowered the floor panel over himself. Right then, the door to the storeroom finally gave.

"Where they go?" yelled one of the 418.

"Check under tables! Check the vents!" another screamed back.

ITm4ster crawled ahead of him, so Greg tried to keep up in the narrow space. He grunted as he felt the scratch of metal brackets holding the mess of power and IT cables in place, along with their glowing indicator lights, and wondered briefly what would happen if one of the wires were to give him a shock down below. Better that he didn't think about that now.

--FOLLOW ME--, the display on his glasses read. Curiouser and curiouser indeed. And this guy, ITm4ster or whatever the hell his real name was, was leading him down the proverbial and somewhat literal rabbit hole. They made another turn in the darkness, and Greg could just hear the sounds of gunfire punctuated by the crunch of plastic. The guards finally decided they had to be hiding beneath the floor panelling.

They came out into another room, though this one seemed to be a server room of some kind. Racks all around hummed with the flickering of green and blue LEDs, giving off the room's illumination. Removing his borrowed glasses, Greg realised a backup generator must be powering the server racks during the recently-induced blackout. He was starting to wonder if he should sabotage the 418's operations by pulling out a couple of racks when ITm4ster reached for one of them.

"Touch not the Devices, for they are sacred to us," said ITm4ster. And right before Greg, he stuck a finger into an ethernet port.

"What are you—" began Greg, but he never finished his sentence. Two of the floor's panels opened in a silent hum, like the wings of a gull beginning to fly. In the hole that formed was revealed a stairway, which formed a square spiral down into a cavern. Glowing veins that resembled the tracts of a circuit board ran into the darkness. Several cables could be seen leading into its depths, and somehow, Greg knew this did not lead to anything that belonged to the 418.

"Follow me," continued ITm4ster in a monotone, but Greg stopped him with a hand.

"Hang on," he said. "Just who the hell are you? And where are you taking me?"

"Such little time, and yet so many questions!" breathed ITm4ster and Greg can't help but wonder if such a voice could belong to a person. "I am your saviour and guarantor. Without me, you would have but perished in the place from which we left. Dally any longer, and we will surely be discovered. For though this room is but part of the 418, not so is our sanctum down below. Either follow, or leave."

With that, ITm4ster stepped inside the hole.

INTO THE RABBIT HOLE

G‍REG FIGURED THAT nothing could possibly be worse than a neo-triad on your heels with MP5s and an assortment of SAR 21s. With all the options laid out like that, the choice was obvious. But who in the world actually spoke in that corny way of ITm4ster's? It wasn't like many people read books before The Storm. He stepped slowly into the stairway, and hefted hard at the doors to close them after him. They wouldn't budge.

"The doors close by themselves. The Cloud acts on its own whims and fancies," came ITm4ster's voice. Shaking off the creepiness all this was giving him, Greg stepped onwards. Every step he made on the plastic material—at least, he guessed it was plastic—illuminated some form of light source beneath, adding a light blue glow to his steps. This was just so ... Tron. He had watched that old classic with his family back when they still had a home to call their own, and too much about this abyss he was descending into was in the realm of science fiction.

He reached the bottom of the stairs—which had to be at least six storeys down. ITm4ster stood waiting for him. Looking around, Greg couldn't see any sign of a door, or any other point of entry.

"Acolyte ITm4ster to enter the Sanctum," droned ITm4ster.

"What?" asked Greg.

"Access not granted," came an electronic feminine voice. "Unidentified lifeform detected. Guest or foe?" A flat monotone, it carried neither warmth nor suspicion.

"Requesting Guest Application 248-34," answered ITm4ster. "Submitting Guarantor Protocol 958-23." As he spoke, Greg could see him drawing his fingers over parts of his skull. A subdermal Wi-Fi connection?

"Access granted. Welcome, Acolyte." Hydraulic actuators hissed as a heavy segment of steel composite was lifted from its perch, high-efficiency electric motors barely humming in the silence. ITm4ster nodded once to the stunned Greg before stepping within.

The corridors they entered had the walls of some kind of metal, of what colour Greg couldn't tell, given the ambient illumination provided on the ceiling above. The glowing tracts he had seen made their way through the ceiling above, alternating between green and blue. Looking closely at the walls as he followed his guide, Greg realised it was inscribed with thousands upon thousands of ones and zeros. Binary code. The fundamentals of all digital computing and communication. Running a hand over it, he found that the numbers were not cast, but chiselled, stamped, or otherwise engraved onto the surface. What significance do these numbers present? Do they speak of source code long since lost with The Storm, or did it show pathways to server directories only the digital or mentally-inclined could make sense of? Greg wanted to stay, but ITm4ster was far ahead by now. Who knew what might happen were he to be found unaccompanied by anyone else here.

Greg needn't have worried. Not a soul could be seen in the

corridors they passed. The doorways he passed were all open, and it was only upon closer inspection that he realised they had no doors to speak off. He caught glimpses of what looked like small server rooms, except that they were hooked up to all manners of display meters and paraphernalia that would give any layman who tried making sense of it a brain tumour. There also appeared to be what looked like sleeping areas, only that the beds were situated next to a mess of wired connectors and equipment that may have once belonged to a hospital.

"Where is everybody?" asked Greg. The acolyte continued walking, the faint unnatural light of the surroundings glinting off his skin. Sometime after they had entered the sanctum, ITm4ster had discarded his lab coat. Beneath it, he was wearing a white shirt and pants, which caught the ambient light well.

"The Brothers are currently attending a sermon by the Administrator," he replied. "I must ask that when we go in attendance, you are not to interrupt them in any way, for such an affront in the Inner Sanctum will hardly be tolerated. Also, let me make the introductions." ITm4ster stopped at a section of wall. Somehow, Greg wasn't overly surprised. Nothing here resembled normal architectural standards.

"I seek to breach the Firewall, and partake in the Vastness of The Cloud!" ITm4ster spoke with his head bowed. With a click, the section of wall lifted.

A rhythmical chanting could be heard the moment the hidden door was open, and Greg could feel the chills down his spine as he followed ITm4ster. Darker than much of the corridor he had just come from, the passageway resembled the entrance to many of the auditoriums and theatres Greg had been to before The Storm. In fact, Greg could see the marks where a signboard demanding that all phones be turned off would have been. The moment he stepped out into the source of the sound, Greg knew he would never be witness to such a sight anywhere else in the wasteland.

Seated in a half-circle on elevated seats on both sides of where they entered were numerous cultists, all swaying to the rhythm of the chant that reverberated throughout the Sanctum. All looked as geeky, if not more so, than ITm4ster, with oversized goggles resembling the ones he had worn. Some had hoods, while those who didn't revealed hair that grew each and every other way. Each one of them had a wire trailing into the back of their necks, which swayed with the movement of their hosts. The chants consisted of intonations of various sounds, including gasps, clicks, and even a chittering that sounded like telephone feedback. This was interspersed with several invocations by the leader of the congregation.

"... and it is through the Code that we exist, and through the Script that we live and prosper!" extolled the priest. Older than the other devotees, he had a white beard that glowed blue in the ambient light, tied once around his neck. From his lectern, a cable likewise trailed into the back of his head. "For it is only through ones and zeros that all things come into being! So be it said!"

"So be it said!" chorused the congregation. They swayed together like a wave, or in Greg's mind, like stalks of grass.

"Long had it been foreseen by Father Jobs, and Father Gates! For only when we are connected can we be part of the greater World!" roared the priest. "And only then can the World have a part of us!"

"As they had said and so foreseen," chanted the followers. "The Internet of Things was but the beginning, Transcendence is the start to the End ..."

The priest raised his hands slowly and deliberately, and a hush quickly fell over the congregation. The clicks and chirps died away.

"Why have you brought an outsider in our midst?" asked the priest with only the slightest tilt of his head. Despite not looking towards the newcomers, there was no doubt he was speaking to ITm4ster. Now that he was turned towards them, Greg could see he had a tattoo that resembling a data tract across his face and exposed parts of his hands. His tattoos and threads of his robe glowed with an otherworldly light, and Greg wondered if there was ultraviolet light integrated into the room's lighting, or something else entirely.

"Forgive my trespass, Administrator!" spoke ITm4ster. "In the midst of danger to my life, it had come to me that this man's life be saved."

"Just as unintended code births forth a virus, unwanted intruders harbour discord and danger," hummed the priest, and miraculously, all manner of weapons appeared in the cultists' hands. Even as he whipped out his own revolver, Greg could also hear the signatory squeal of an electronic control weapon being readied.

"Peace! I ask for peace!" squawked ITm4ster, throwing himself before Greg, even as the cultists stood and chanted. The Administrator himself held what appeared to be an enormous water gun, but the cult's fervour confirmed its far more deadly intent.

"Speak forth your reason for trespass, intruder!" demanded the Administrator as he stepped forward, cerebral cable trailing behind. "That, or 20,000 volts await you!" He resumed chanting a verse of his own.

"Put your guns down first!" yelled Greg. His hands shook as

he gripped the scratched grip of his revolver.

"What the Admin says, you follow," said a voice behind him. "Do so, or be erased." A loud click came from behind Greg's head, and he didn't need to turn to know it was the sound of a shotgun being racked.

The incredulity of what he had seen since entering the sanctum would have had Greg in hysterics if it weren't for his time in the mines and the wasteland. In the wasteland, he had seen people commit atrocities to each other for the simplest of resources. He had seen gangs of bikers riding the broken highways of Johor in the hope of finding what was left of their old hangouts, burning precious fuel for a lost cause. So what was there to stop a bunch of computer freaks from falling in their own flights of fancy, and worship computerised code as their Gods? His Taurus 85 dropped to the floor with a clatter, barely visible upon the dark floor. One of the cultists stepped forward to take it.

"Let us adjourn our communion to a more uncertain time," said the Administrator, lowering his weapon. "Your intervention is most welcome, Wesley. Please take the intruder to the Quarantine Folder. I need to have a word with you, Acolyte IT," he added to ITm4ster.

A prod from a shotgun muzzle gave Greg all the impetus he needed to get going. Going straight through the sanctum, a door opened automatically, and Greg stepped into a corridor he hadn't been in. Not that it made much difference, given its similarity to the others. He chanced a look back as he walked.

"Eyes to the front!" snapped Wesley, and a jab of the gun barrel had Greg facing the front once more, but not before he got a good look at his escort. About his age, Wesley looked nothing like any of the other crackpots he had seen in this joint. His goggles resembled the old SAF ballistic goggles, suggesting it was directed more towards protection than digital immersion. His hair was cut shorter and he wore a T-shirt and cargo pants, above which were pouches which probably contained devices of an offensive nature. His confident posture and grip of his gun not unlike that of the few garang soldiers he had observed back in the army suggested a more physical background. Greg was glad he hadn't tried resisting. This guy had the skill to take him out in an instant, and maybe even tweet or post about it in whatever application or LAN network this place had.

Greg had expected a door that functioned somewhat similarly to the ones he had seen earlier, but "Quarantine Folder" appeared to be a glorified name for a cell. Sure, Wesley tapped his head to wirelessly unlock the door, but it still swung upon hinges, just like any other.

Greg entered the room, and saw that it was partitioned in three different sections: the walkway, which he was now in, and a cell on each side. The Quarantine Folder had none of the splendour of the glowing circuitry of the walls and flooring Greg had seen earlier. Instead of proper prison bars, metal mesh had been welded, tied, or otherwise held together to make up the cell door and walls.

"Get into the cell on your right," commanded Wesley, and Greg complied. He just had time to see an old bench and a bucket making up the only contents of the room before Wesley slid the grate to the cell shut.

"Should you try to escape, or otherwise hurt our flock, I will personally delete you," warned Wesley. His face betrayed no expression whatsoever. "That is your final warning." Before Greg could ask him to elaborate what "delete" meant, the well-armed computer cultist left, electronic door clicking shut.

Okay. These guys were officially whack. As whack as anyone could be post-Storm. All Greg had left to do was wait for the Admin to come and say his piece. He may have found out what experiments were taking place in the 418 IT labs, but Greg still didn't know where Jin was. He shuddered briefly as he thought about what he had seen on the clipboard affixed to the cage. Implanting data connectors to a person was one thing, but doing it to children? But then, the triads weren't known for doing things the right way. Not even before The Storm. Even their hazing rituals were pretty intense stuff.

A pair of eyes glinted at him from the opposite cell and Greg turned quickly. It was the kid he had seen in the IT labs. What was his name again? Guo Li.

"How did you get in here?" hissed Greg.

"When you were holding the guy in the white coat against the cage, I took his keys," said Guo Li. "The men with guns went away, so I unlocked my cage and followed them. After they left the room you ran into, I found the way you had gone. There was an opening on the floor, so I went in.

Then some funny-looking guy with big goggles took me to this room."

Greg leaned his head against the mesh. This was no place for kids. Or any sane person, for that matter. "Did the guy in the white coat do anything bad to you?" he asked.

Guo Li thought for a moment. Those drugs he had been fed must be doing their job. "No. He talks a bit weird, actually quite good to me. The other people shout and sometimes beat me, but he doesn't. Sometimes, he look like he doesn't know whether to do something or not." He looked closely at Greg. "You have children?"

Greg sat back against the wall of the cell. "Yes."

"One of them is called Jin?" asked Guo Li, beating out a rhythm on the mesh. "What games does he know how to play?"

Greg wanted to yell back at the kid, and tell him that the world was completely fucked up, and one was extremely lucky if one had time to consider taking a breath. But as he looked into the glints that made up Guo Li's eyes, he realised that he really wasn't much different from Jin in age. Thrown into the mess of the world before they could even contemplate the seriousness of it all, Guo Li might have experienced some of the horrors Jin had.

"He didn't play much," said Greg. "Back in the Mines, he would sometimes draw things in the sand, so you could say he's an artist. Before The Storm, he said he wanted to design computers."

"What are computers?"

Greg stared at Guo Li for a moment before realising that the kid was too young to have known what computers or smartphones were when The Storm happened. It was strange really, then back before The Storm, smartphones and tablets were so commonplace that even young children had their eyes and hands glued to them for most of the day. Some parents had even stuck tablets in baby prams. Greg had found that utterly fucked up in more ways than one. In a way, The Storm had done some good by resetting the bad habits of the past, but Greg doubted the enslavement of hundreds upon thousands of people was worth it all.

"They're devices that show you information you can see or read," said Greg.

"Like books?"

"No, they're not the same thing. Look, I'll tell you more later if we have time. Where were you from?"

Guo Li beat out a rhythm on the mesh. "Why do you want

to know?" he asked. A cautious kid. His parents had taught him well.

"Well, you need to get back to your Ma and Pa. Otherwise, they're going to be worried about you," said Greg. The irony of the two layers of mesh between them wasn't lost, but he didn't intend to sit still when his captors arrived.

"They're both dead," answered Guo Li. Greg stiffened.

"I'm sorry, kid," replied Greg. But words were just that—words.

"It's alright," Guo Li sighed. "When it happened, I felt really sad. But Uncle Kim Shang said they died for their country, so it is okay. If they died caring only for themselves, then it's not. But then, if I didn't follow some of his guys, I wouldn't kena caught. So now I dunno what is correct."

Greg mused on this for a second. "Your uncle allowed you to follow him?" he asked doubtfully.

Guo Li's eyes dipped. "He didn't," whispered the kid. "When he goes on missions, I follow from far. He never sees me."

"Why did you? The world is dangerous."

"I want to be like Mama and Papa. I want to serve the country," Guo Li stuck his chin out defiantly. "Uncle said I cannot, but if we don't all do our part, how can our country become strong? So I follow them, learn what they do. But then they suddenly have to run. I was too slow to catch up with them, and then the guys with many tattoos caught me. They're very scary, one guy even beat me." Guo Li showed the bruises on his cheek. "But this guy, I think he's some sort of leader, he said they need keep me healthy. Then they locked me in the cage, next to other kids. I tried to talk to them, but they don't feel like it. One even told me to go and die. When the guys in white coats came, one by one, they took them away. A few days later, you came."

Greg scratched his head, settling himself against the mesh. All this was interesting, but didn't tell him much about the situation. He was just about to clarify where Guo Li was actually from when the door to the cells hummed open. The Admin entered, followed by Wesley.

Now that he was up close, Greg could see the Admin had the hood of his robe drawn back to expose his head and neck. Across his skin were markings that resembled the circuitry one could see on pre-Storm electronics, accentuated by his whitish hair. Greg was wondering if they were simply tattoos, or served some higher function when the Admin spoke.

"My acolyte told me of the circumstances leading to your chance meeting," spoke the Admin. There wasn't any noticeable accent to place his ethnicity, and Greg wondered if all cultists had received some form of speech implant. "He stated that despite the defences the heretics above had in place to their labs, you managed to find your way in. It was clear you were not there for the treasures they hold, but for someone else. Who may that be?"

Greg kept mum, staring back into the Admin's eyes. It seemed to glow slightly as the cult leader spoke.

"Listen, outsider. The only ones welcome here are those who worship the Code in some way. The reason why you haven't been deleted like protocol dictates is because ITm4ster believes you have skills that could prove useful." The Admin leaned in closer. "But your outward hostility has me wondering about the danger you pose to the Code, along with my acolyte's judgement. So how about you answer my questions, and prove just how beneficial you are to our cause?"

Greg could always spit back at him. But when he thought about it, this Brotherhood, or Fraternity, or whatever else they were hadn't done him any harm. If anything, he was the trespasser. They could have stunned him with one of their electroshock weapons—assuming they actually worked—before throwing him into this glorified cell. And they had taken the risk of harbouring him. Unlike the triads, these people didn't seem to be living under the heel of an oppressive power. They were minding their own business, right until he came along.

"I'm looking for my son," Greg finally said. "He was taken less than two weeks back. I heard he might have been in the labs."

The Admin drew his head back, his face creased into a frown. "Your son? Perhaps you should start from the beginning." Wesley looked on wordlessly.

Greg didn't know why these guys needed to know about his own personal quest. But he had barged into whatever counted as a holy refuge for them. Anywhere else in the wasteland, it would have been "shoot first, ask later". But a group like this couldn't have built their sanctum without the right know-how. They likely had connections to places throughout the country, the 418 even, as ITm4ster had proven. And so he told them how he came to be there. His time in the mines, his journey through the MRT tunnels, the deal he had made with Lantern.

The Admin scratched his chin when he was done. They didn't even seem fazed by the ferals in the tunnels. "What do you think about all that, Wesley?" he muttered.

"There *is* a 93.79 percent probability of his telling the truth," said Wesley. Wesley maintained his composure even when speaking to his Admin.

"I know that, Guardian," snorted the Admin. "If I need numbers, I can consult my own sensors. I was asking if you believe our visitor can help us towards our ultimate goal."

"He does seem rather composed, for a wastelander," commented Wesley. "He will definitely be of greater help than the average Brother."

"Help you with what?" Greg narrowed his eyes. "And before we even start, to whom do I have the pleasure of speaking?"

The Admin looked back at Greg. "I am the leader of my flock, the keeper of the Digital Verse. My username is 1 and 127, the beginning and the end. For it was I who started this sanctuary, and without I it shall fall. Many of my followers have cast aside their analogue lives for want of a digital salvation. It was only through a great undertaking on our part that this became possible. We are the Brotherhood of the Code, seekers of Binary Truth."

"I'm puzzled how you managed to carve out a space right under the 418's HQ," mused Greg. "Did you both have an arrangement?"

The Admin's eyes flashed. "Sacrilege! We have no dealings with the likes of those defilers!"

"But your acolyte—"

"ITm4ster? He was our Trojan in the system! How else could we have rerouted the power the Heretics hang so greedily onto? He feeds us news on their actions and plans. So that we may bide our time to strike. But now that his cover is all but blown," the Admin eyed Greg critically, "it seems that you owe us."

"Owe you?" asked Greg incredulously. "I didn't ask to be saved!"

"Then we should throw you back out," suggested the Admin. "In bit strings even, if necessary.

The outlaws of the 418 shouldn't become ours."

"Admin, if I may make bold, perhaps I can speak to the outsider?" Wesley ventured as Greg and the Admin glared at each other. He had taken off his goggles, and beneath it, Greg could see the indentations the goggles had made. Rings of pink could barely be seen on slightly tanned skin, confirming that Wesley did go topside every now and then. He had to be no older than 32 at the most, yet his eyes carried that professionalism Greg recognised in those independent types. His eyes were far from hard, but neither were they the orbs of a starry-eyed student fresh out of university.

"Say your piece, Guardian."

"As you have probably discerned from your brief time here, few of us here are operationally inclined," said Wesley. Unlike the other acolytes, he gestured with both hands and head, his eyebrows enunciating what he said. "I am but one of the few who have skills beyond the ways of the Code. There is a situation in which your skills would be of help to us."

"And what makes you think I have these skills?" demanded Greg. "Sure, I may have broken into the labs, but I'm just an ordinary guy."

"Not so by our observations," affirmed the Admin. "Softwareanalysis confirms your confidence in ranged and close combat, well beyond that of the average 49er soldier. Furthermore, ITm4ster was first-hand witness to your manhandling of him. Close combat techniques right out of SAF Documentation MSD-3138-3A! If you hadn't told us who you were, I'll say you were from the Old Guard."

"I wasn't from Guards or ADF," snorted Greg. "If your all-knowing software is so great, you would have been able to tell I was from 6AMB. That's under Combat Maintenance."

The Admin looked livid, his hand reaching into his robes. Wesley cleared his throat.

"You're really out of touch with the world, aren't you?" he

said quickly. "We weren't talking about units or formations. Not that they exist anymore, mind. Not unless you consider the last remnants banding together in the vicinity of City Hall. The Old Guard are the last surviving contingent of the SAF."

"The task, Wesley!" said the Admin sharply.

"Very well, Admin. We can talk about current affairs later," said Wesley. "The point is, I suspect we know where your son is."

Greg gripped the mesh of his cell. "Don't lie to me."

"According to ITm4ster, several children were subjected to tests in the labs you were in," continued Wesley. "Now, though ITm4ster was not involved in the higher-level planning of such experiments, he knows that the children had been sent to a server facility some distance from here."

"Server?" said Greg. Then his face contorted. "You're lying!"

"Why would we be?" asked the Admin. "We aren't the ones with something to lose."

"All the servers were destroyed during The Storm!" roared Greg. "We all saw what it could do, even our buildings weren't safe from it! And you expect me to believe that of all places, a working server facility still exists upon our sunny island? Speak of it in your gospel, if you will, but leave me the fuck out of it!"

"It is really so difficult to believe?" asked Wesley, and the calm tone he projected caused Greg to turn back towards him. "In the 21st century, our country was at the forefront of science and technology. We had research facilities dedicated to the study of every field. We built structures no one had thought possible. We invented the first flash drive.

What few people know is that we have a data bank right beneath Gardens by the Bay and Marina Barrage. It is where the last of the world's data is stored. The "sustainable ecosystem" at

Gardens by the Bay? The damming system at nearby Marina Barrage? It's all built to power and cool it."

"And the 418 controls it," said Greg. "What has this got to do with my son?"

Wesley and the Admin looked at each other. "He and the other children may have been brought there to unlock the server system with their neural implants."

It took a half minute for the facts to sink in. "Let me out of here!" Greg snarled, kicking and thrashing against his prison. A sizable dent formed on the mesh where the Admin's face was, and he noted with some satisfaction that the cult leader flinched.

"Initiate Pacification Protocol," ordered the Admin. He maintained his composure even as Greg thrashed and bashed against his cell.

"Admin?"

"Do it."

"Fuck your pacification ritual! Fuck you all! Let me out!" screamed Greg. He didn't care if they thought he was an animal; all he wanted was to go rescue his son from those whoresons that called themselves the 418. They will pay for what they have done, they will suffer for long and terrible moments—

Two jets of gas sprayed out of the cell walls over him. Emitting several large chokes, Greg collapsed, blurry images of two figures flashing past. What looked like a child looked on, even as he gave one final wheeze.

JOURNEYING FORTH

GREG'S EYES FELT puffy. He would gladly sleep for a few hours more, but something told him it would be a bad idea. He had to reach someplace, somewhere. Try as he might, he could not remember where. What work detail was he on? Shaft Crew? Excavation? He rolled to his side, expecting to drop his feet to the floor.

He felt the characteristic pitch in his stomach as he fell, awaking with a shock. Smooth and cool, the surface he was on felt nothing like any place in the mines.

"Don't worry. You're fine," said a voice. Greg flinched, looking around wildly. The room was lit by a soft white lighting, which reflected off the smooth white of the tiles. He blinked his eyes hard, struggling to make sense of it. Ahead of him was a figure dressed in white, along with another in dull colours.

"Take deep breaths, it'll be a short while before the endorphins are flushed out of your system," said the voice. It sounded familiar. "How're you feeling?"

He wasn't in the mines. No one gave a shit about anyone in there. If you fell sick, the enforcers sent a slave crew to drag you out to a containment area. There, you were left with the other sick and wounded. Only water would be provided. At the end of each day, an enforcer would come by and prod each body with his club. If you looked well enough to work, you would return back to your duties. If you weren't, but still showed signs of life, he would leave you till the next day.

For those who didn't respond ... Greg heard the tales. A crew would take them to the exit and have them buried. This way, no one escaped by playing sick. No medical care of any sort was given, unless you knew someone with folk knowledge. And their help always came with a price.

For someone to ask how he was feeling, he was anywhere but there.

"I can't see shit," mumbled Greg. He blinked hard, and yet his vision remained blurry.

"Alright, adjusting sensory inputs," mumbled the white figure. Greg felt his vision gradually getting sharper, almost like adjusting the focus knob on a pair of binoculars. He blinked twice, and saw ITm4ster and Wesley before him.

"Feeling better?" asked ITm4ster. Unlike the guy he had met back in the 418 labs, the ex- infiltrator now wore the robes of his order. Strapped to his waist was a device that appeared to be some sort of signal interface, with graphs and readings pulsing in several sections.

"Yeah," Greg tottered slightly as he sat upright. "What happened, anyway?"

Wesley and ITm4ster looked at each other. "You were unconscious. So we treated you." It was then Greg realised he had wires attached to him. These led to an oscilloscope that had been pilfered right out of a polytechnic, with its inventory control label still affixed. Upon his arm was a tube that was fed with some fluid from a drip bag. Within the same room was another foldout bed with two tanks of oxygen nearby. He was in a sick bay. A pretty high-tech sick bay, in wasteland terms.

"Treated me?" Greg realised he was supposed to be angry about something, but somehow, he felt airy, calm even. "I don't see any meds around. What did you use?"

"Most symptoms of the body can be interpreted as the direct result of chemical imbalances within," said ITm4ster. He spoke with the smooth voice and confidence of a doctor. "Responses are also triggered by brain signals, which are little more than electrical pulses. I had therefore adjusted them within the average parameters."

"You were messing around in my head?" said Greg in alarm. So that's what all these wires were for. He fumbled with them, despite ITm4ster's protests. "Are you even a real doctor?"

"Count yourself lucky, outsider," growled Wesley. "ITm4ster had a minor in Biological Systems before The Storm. You've just undergone treatment only our order is privy to. If it weren't for the auspices of the Admin, we would leave you out for the 418."

"What did you guys gas me with anyway?" snorted Greg. The probes were too difficult to remove, so he let ITm4ster pluck them out. "That was rather high-handed."

"A non-toxic concoction. Things being as they were, you weren't in any state for conversation. If nothing else, the rest would have done you some good," said Wesley. He didn't look at all perturbed. ITm4ster proceeded to draw a surgical tube out of Greg's arm.

"How long was I out?"

"Close to nine hours."

"The fuck!" Greg jerked forward. "You mean I lost half a day sleeping it out?"

"You came to our sanctum at two in the morning. It's eleven

now," said Wesley. "And may I remind you that you weren't in any state to continue? Not just in terms of anger management, but fatigue and malnourishment. The rest and IV drip helped with that. Besides, the Admin is more than willing to resume where we left off." The acolyte jerked his head to the door. "Shall we?"

Greg felt he should be angry about being gassed and put through questionable medical procedures without his consent. But much as he hated to admit it, he felt far better than he ever had. Perhaps it was the long-needed rest, or even the unorthodox treatment he had been subjected to. With a nod to ITm4ster, Greg followed Wesley out.

The corridor was lit the same way as the night before, only that the colour of the light source was now a pale yellow rather than dark blue. A day-night simulation program, if Greg was to hazard a guess. A passing acolyte bowed as they passed, but Greg didn't hold any fantasies of it being accorded to him. Up ahead was a door set in the side; Greg recognised it as the entrance to the cell room. For a moment, he thought he would be put inside the cell again, but Wesley remotely opened the door opposite it.

Like the cell room, this one held none of the frills evident in the corridors or congregation hall. A bare plastic table stood in the centre of the room, with the Admin sitting at the head of it. On the right was what looked to be a two-way mirror looking into a room identical to the one they were in. On closer look, the scene beyond appeared grainy, confirming it was actually a wall-to-wall monitor display. With a start, Greg saw that the kid was seated alone at a table. What appeared to be electronic entertainment devices including a pair of augmented reality googles were scattered throughout its surface. Guo Li did not pay them any attention, however, choosing instead to hug his legs close to his chest, humming a tune that could be heard through the speakers.

"Good morning, Greg," greeted the Admin, and Greg turned back towards him. "I trust you had a good rest? Have a seat."

"It appears so, Admin," said Greg. He could see a faded A*STAR label on the back of his chair as he pulled it out. "It wasn't like I had any choice in the matter."

The Admin smiled. "We all do, Greg. And every action begets a reaction. You will find that much of the wasteland would be more brutal in meeting out justice. As long as we're on the same screen, I'm sure you'll forgive us for our trespass." The cult leader inclined his head.

"I guess."

"Good. It appears that the two of us have our own set of goals. The 418 have your son. They also have in their control an ultra-high capacity server farm. As you can see, my flock are not fighters. We'll gladly take up arms to defend our beliefs, but are best suited to pursuing the way of the Code."

"Really." Greg chanced a look at Wesley. The Guardian merely looked back.

"Wesley is an outlier, and like you, he had also been trained in the arts of war. Before The Storm, he hailed from 9th Signal Battalion, the key communications arm of the SAF. It was his own pursuit of the Code that led him to us after the Crash laid waste to everything. There are few of those alive capable of decrypting the coded radio frequency we broadcasted, and yet he had. We would have been discovered by the 418 if it weren't in part due to his fortifying of the place. From time to time, he and ITm4ster get us what we need from the outside."

"What is this place, actually?" said Greg, looking around. "How can the 418 not know it exists?"

The Admin's eyes flared. "It is a gift from the Code! One does not question it."

"You expect me to—"

"Leave it, Greg," said Wesley, and Greg was surprised at his calmness. "Our ways are not privy to those outside it. The Admin's only wish is to protect his flock."

"Anyway," the Admin's voice now carried an edge, "I know that the 418 had discovered the server no more than a year back. One of their excavation runs of the Barrage area must have yielded it. From what I gather, despite having physical access to the server, they've been unable to get past the encryption. Transporting the children there suggests they have need for organic intervention. As I had mentioned in our last meeting, it is possible they're experimenting on neural interfacing."

As far as Greg knew, bio-electronic interfacing didn't exist even in the year leading up to The Storm. It wasn't possible for the simple reason that the precise electrical signals from electronics weren't directly compatible with the random impulses of an organic mind. He had read an article in a tech magazine about local researchers in A*STAR extolling the wide potential such a study would have, but that was the last of it. Like everything else, the theory and tech behind it was lost during The Storm.

Until now. It seemed the 418 was as resourceful as a criminal organisation could ever get.

"Then I have no time to waste," said Greg. "I need to go get my son." He made to get up.

"A place of such value is unlikely to be easily breached, even for one with your capabilities," said the Admin. He didn't look at all perturbed. "If you think you've seen the best of the 418, you're sorely mistaken. Their most hardened enforcers will be guarding it, along with the best military equipment available in the region. Tell me, Greg: all in all, how much do you know about computers?

"I know enough."

"Are you familiar with any of the Script?" pressed the Admin. "C++? Java? SQL?" Greg stared back at him. "I thought not. Even if you somehow make it to the mother lode intact, you won't be able to do anything with the server. If your son is plugged in, extracting him without disengaging the protocols will be fatal. My Champion, Guardian Wesley, will aid you in your quest."

Greg knew what the Admin was saying. "What's in it for you?" he asked. The simplest and truest rule in the wasteland. When the world went to hell, with it went the Courtesy Lion, and whatever had counted as social norms. If anyone gave you a favour, it was never for free. Quid pro quo, as the phrase went.

"For years we have lived within our sanctum, rarely venturing forth," spoke the Admin. "Not because we fear the outside world, but because of my followers' limitations. We may be versed in the Code, and possess far more knowledge than most other factions in the wasteland. But my followers need more than the comfort of the Code to ground them. This may be our Sanctum, but some are questioning whether it is no more than a place of worship. The data our intranet holds can only occupy curious minds for so long. They need a place in which they can be in greater communion of, a holy site, if you will. When we occupy the server, my flock will find deeper meaning in directory after directory of information. They will devote their lives to the curation of vast amounts of data, so that it may live on even in The Cloud."

All this sounded like the wild fantasies of a deranged maniac. "So you want control of the server, is that right?" confirmed Greg. "What are you going to do with it?"

"Preserve the data for all eternity. Help it find its way to The Cloud!" The Admin's voice came out close to a moan. "So that we'll be blessed forevermore by the Code. Only then can we achieve Transcendence!"

A silence descended upon the room, and Greg's eyes flitted to the two cultists. They both had a look of fervour upon their faces, smiles stretched in anticipation.

"Very well, then," said Greg, finally breaking the silence. "It appears we have mutually aligned goals. The Server for Wesley's assistance. So how do we get there? Do we walk?"

"The journey to the digital gardens is long and far," declared the Admin. "And you do not have long to tarry. The Old City is extremely dangerous, come nightfall. I will have transportation arranged for you immediately." The Admin closed his eyes for a moment. "It's been done. Wesley will show you where to go."

As Greg rose from his seat with the two Codists, his eyes fell on the screen-window. Guo Li stood looking towards them, almost as if he could see Greg. His face was impassive, and yet Greg couldn't help wondering about the kid. He took life as it came, unquestioning even when his parents died. Even now, trapped in a place he didn't know, all he did was exhibit a mild curiosity. But what would happen once the Brotherhood got into his head? This wasn't a place to bring up a child. He would lose his childhood, and turn into a techno-religious nut whose beliefs knew no limits.

"What's the kid doing there?" asked Greg, jerking his head towards the screen.

The Admin turned and sighed. "An interesting test of our defences he proved to be. Wesley found him in the corridors shortly after your arrival. He must have bypassed our defences somehow. From what I understand from ITm4ster, he was coming up on the test list of the 418 IT research department, but has yet to receive Implantation. Good scores in mental calculations and cognitive reasoning. With his aptitude, I am sure he would make a good member of the flock."

"He's coming with me," said Greg. The Admin looked at Greg strangely, even as Wesley froze.

"You're in no position to tell us what to do, Greg," reminded the Admin. "Besides which, you're hardly equipped to handle a child in the open. Remember that you have a son to rescue."

"I've spoken to the kid. He knows the area," lied Greg. "He used to accompany his uncle out during his duties. This is a critical mission, and we could use all of the help we can get. Once the 418 knows ITm4ster's missing, the area's going to be fortified tighter than MINDEF back in the day. Ways to get around them will be most welcome."

"You aren't going to deprive us a member of the fold," huffed the Admin, and Greg could see his tattoos glowing red. "Few are worthy of the Code, and even fewer available to join us."

"Will you really trade a holy site all for the sake of one more disciple?" asked Greg. He knew he was pushing his luck, and the Admin could at any moment being his whole cult down upon him, Wesley included. "When word goes round that the Brotherhood had helped the server come online, drove after drove would flock to you for your guidance! You would be revered for your insight, and the Code will live on in the hearts of many! But this, Admin, can only happen if we succeed. And we need the kid for that."

The Admin was silent, staring hard into Greg's eyes. His in-built social analysis software was probably running at full capacity, trying to see past the bullshit Greg was trying to pull. He must either have injected enough truth into his words, or been a really smooth liar, because the cult leader finally nodded.

"So be it said," said the Admin, and Greg could see his tattoos reverting to blue. "Let it not be said that the Code does not live in the hearts of others! Wesley, go with Greg and get the youngster. May the Code light your path."

Greg was almost surprised that worked. Without making eye contact with the Admin, he followed Wesley to the next room.

The moment Greg entered the room, it was apparent that it was meant more for observation rather than incarceration. Some form of air-conditioning could be felt, keeping the room at a comfortable temperature. Guo Li looked up at the newcomers, blinking slightly. He didn't seem at all worried, but it could always be a front.

"Come on, kid. The Admin says you're coming with us," said Wesley, not unkindly.

Guo Li tilted his head. "Oh! Where to?" He looked happy, for someone who was in a strange new place.

"The Marina Bay area," confirmed Greg. "We're going to need your help, but the world out there is dangerous. It's best that you keep close to us—"

"Sian. How come everyone talks to me like this?" complained Guo Li. "Treating me like I don't know anything!" He got up and walked out the door, muttering as he did. Wesley looked briefly at Greg, but the ex-soldier just looked back with raised eyebrows.

"Pretty headstrong, eh?" asked Wesley as they followed quickly, the door humming shut behind them.

"Don't ask me. We've only just met," replied Greg. The kid kept an easy pace ahead of them, and for a moment, Greg wondered if he already knew the way out of here. But he eventually slowed down at a junction, where Wesley took charge.

"You're weird," the kid said to Wesley. The enforcer said nothing.

"That's rude, Guo Li," admonished Greg. What was he doing? This wasn't his kid.

"I'm not. This man is wearing goggles even when he's underground. And he's got wires in his head."

For a moment, Greg almost told Guo Li not to discriminate against people based on their looks and religion. Then he wondered if the software the BOC worshipped actually counted as one in the first place. Sure, to them their divinities presented themselves as ones and zeros, file types of .exe to .xml. But that would mean that he, Greg Lin, along with perhaps eight billion others, conversed with deities each time they typed on their computer or phone. Who was he to judge, anyway? He was no theologist.

Wesley simply chuckled. "It seems we have a talker on our hands."

They passed several acolytes on the way, who, aside from a "Hail, Guardian", didn't do more than look at them. They descended down a stairway that lacked the high-tech appearance of the corridors, composing of mismatched plates of metal and plastic planks, held together by assemblies of bolts and construction scaffolding. It was clear this was a relatively new excavation, and it must have taken some semblance of skill to set up. Not something Greg expected from computer geeks, but they could have easily read a cached Wikihow page or YouTube video to do it. Ten flights of stairs they descended down, with the occasional groan of steel. Just as Greg hoped they didn't have to climb back up another flight of stairs, they came upon a steel door. Here, the air felt almost humid, like it led to the outdoors.

Wesley rapped hard onto it, the gong of metal echoing beyond. Greg looked meaningfully at him.

"This sector's not connected to the Brotherhood's electrical grid," explained Wesley. "Besides, it's far more secure this way."

"What is this place, then?" Greg asked. Guo Li looked impatient to get moving.

"One of the gates to the outside world." The door creaked open. For a moment, he was silhouetted by sunlight, and Greg shielded his eyes. His eyes adjusted slowly, a side effect of having been in the mines for so long.

When Greg broke free of his prison of five years, he could barely keep his eyes open. The sun that shone upon him was both a blessing and a curse, a painful reminder of what he had missed. He had heard of those born underground, whose eyes never saw clearly in the gaze of the sun. But his pupils had readjusted within two days, so that he didn't need a cap shading his eyes all the time. He had seen sights he had never thought he would see, kinds of people he had never known possible. He had sneaked past 418 outposts, escaped pursuit from a biker gang called the Balik Kampung, who, other than their propensity for violence, were little more than overgrown kids who just wanted to find an old haunt that hadn't been razed to the ground.

A difficult task indeed; of all the old rest stops Greg had seen, none had been spared the horrors of the 418. Some were simply torched and abandoned. Some, including one with an A&W, was converted into a village of sorts, where 418 vehicles restocked on supplies and fuel. Greg had managed to pass them without fanfare, the jacket and armband he filched allowed him to pass unnoticed. Having planned his escape, he had stamped a bogus letter with a Minelords stamp, giving him more credability than any other disguise would. As Liang, the 49er at

Woodlands checkpoint mentioned, he only forgot the coloured stamp of the 418 Brotherhood.

Some of the settlements were pretty laid-back, so he could browse whatever they had to offer. As for others, he could tell one would fare badly even if one was a 418. Greg once came upon a place where an old soccer field had been fenced off for a kind of arena bloodsport. At that time, a Red Pole armed with a woodcutter's axe was pitted not against wastelanders, but several other 49ers. Greg had left without even passing through.

But here in the sanctum of the BOC, it was an entirely different realm. Greg lowered his hand. Through the gate, walls of large, broken concrete that had made up part of a building lay in a circle around a small clearing. The ground was smooth featureless cement, without any tiling, so this had to be an old warehouse or storeroom. But what was of most interest was the relic sitting in the centre of it, flanked by an acolyte in grey overalls.

"Is that—?" Greg whistled.

"A Kawasaki Voyager?" Wesley grinned. The other acolyte got up and nodded to them. "That's right. We found a couple of motorbikes in one of the underground carparks nearby. Flooding had gotten to its insides, but N33r here, our resident techy, has made it his life's work to restore them. And here you have it."

Greg ran a hand over the seat, his hand brushing against the cool metal of the engine exhaust pipe below. The seat had been replaced with what looked like seat cushions, held in place by packaging foam reinforced with elastic straps. The metal parts were of a matte texture that he recognised as burnishing from fine-grit sandpaper. He had seen the restored machines used by the 418, but none of them had had such care given to it.

"What about fuel?" asked Greg. As he walked around, he

saw that a sidecar was attached to it. It looked to have been fabricated out of nothing more than a collection of metal shelves bolted together, with a pair of bicycle wheels thrown in to give it mobility. Guo Li made to climb in, but Greg held him back.

"Alcohol-based biofuels," N33r said proudly. "We have a garden and a lab that lets us make the stuff we need. Have the right blend of alcohols, and you'll soon be moving along faster than a lunatic on steroids. It's all renewable too, if you get my meaning."

"That's if the racket of the engine doesn't tell the whole of the 418 where we are," replied Greg.

"Speed is of the essence. We won't stay too long on the roads; the Admin was pretty clear on that," said Wesley. "You have something else for us, N33r?"

"Do I ever," the acolyte said excitedly. Whipping off the cloth draped across a fold-out table, he presented a selection of weapons to the two. Upon it lay two carbine-style weapons with foregrips, as well as a pistol of some sort. With their plastic exteriors, they looked a lot more like Nerf blasters than weapons of war. Both appeared to be bullpup-style carbines based on the SAR 21 MMS, a variant of the SAR 21 with a shorter barrel and mounting rails on the front and top. Mounted upon the top rail of one was what appeared to be a miniaturised GoPro camera, though Greg couldn't see any way to aim with it. The other carbine had a rear and front sight of marked acrylic and a pen nib. The pistol, on the other hand, appeared to be breech-loaded, and was accompanied by plastic-cased 25mm grenades. Greg could see the markings of the PVC pipe used to make them.

"These are the carbine-class Antivirus 2, also known as the AV-2," prattled N33r. "One of my own in-house designs. Lightweight polymer alloy frames, with elastomer dampening in the buttstock. Both are in standard 5.56mm chambering, with self-adjusting breech for quicker cooling and aim compensation. These are but two of many possible configurations. Go ahead, give them a try."

Greg made to check out the one with the GoPro, but Wesley beat him to it. A little annoyed that he didn't get the more advanced-looking weapon, he hefted the one with the acrylic-iron sights. The markings on the acrylic were almost professional-grade, with increments for different ranges, but it still looked too much like a kid's craft project to him. Ammunition came in tin magazines that were still marked with the printing of candy containers used to make them, but were otherwise similar to the specifications of those used by the common M16 rifle. The assortment of worn brass and plastic 5.56mm casings suggested they had been picked off the street and handloaded. The weapon strap consisted of a wide nylon lanyard which still sported the last A*STAR Open House markings.

"That's for Guardian Wesley," said N33r when Greg picked up the grenade launcher. "Admin's orders, but I'm sure you'll find the AV-2 more than adequate."

"You ever tested these things?" asked Greg, wondering if these lumps of plastic would crumble, or worse, blow apart after a few shots.

N33r looked offended. "Of course! All the simulations tested out fine."

Computer simulations were one thing, field testing was another thing altogether. Greg had had plenty of first-hand experience in the Army. "You have any of the real stuff, like actual SAR 21s? An M16, perhaps?" he asked.

N33r frowned. "You wound me! What I make is as good as anything from any factory! You're more than welcome to go do your own shopping." He grabbed Greg's gun by the foregrip, making to snatch it back. Greg growled, fighting against his pull.

"You guys are very childish leh," commented Guo Li. He had seated himself on the lip of the motorcycle carriage, his legs swinging forward and back.

"Greg, I understand your concern, but I have used N33r's weapons before," cut in Wesley. "In some ways, they are far better than the mass-produced stuff you are used to. Your retina and arm coordination values have already been accounted for and zeroed to your specifications. And they are far lighter than lumps of steel. Sorry, N33r, but you know how outsiders can be."

"Indeed," huffed N33r. "I ought to reconfigure his trigger and bolt group to—"

"He gets the point," said Wesley quickly, slinging his AV-2 across his back. "Get in the carriage with the kid, Greg. So, N33r, we ride directly out through here?"

"As soon as you're ready," confirmed N33r. He ran a hand reverently over the handlebars of the bike, his face inscrutable. "I've just sent you the user guide. Take good care of Beatrice, will you? You're off to do the warrior's work, and I don't want her killed in the process."

"One can never tell," said Wesley. The side carriage was cramped, but had enough space for Greg to sit side-by-side with Guo Li. The seat was better than expected—made of Styrofoam packaging moulded into shape. Bag straps with clips made up the seat belt, and Greg put them around Guo Li and himself, along with two swimming goggles N33r provided. Wesley revved the bike into gear, and it pulled forward with a purr.

So this heap of junk actually worked. For a moment, Greg wondered why Wesley was driving towards a net of rebar. Then the rebar slanted at an angle with the creak of gears, and the bike zipped over it.

They were in mid-air.

Greg yelled, gripping hard on Guo Li's hand as he squealed. For a brief moment, Greg could see the surrounding post-Storm buildings, with their broken facades no tourist would ever want selfies with. Then they landed onto the hard tarmac, and Greg's teeth clattered together. The suspension on the bike was souped up good, and they bounced quickly back to a comfortable rhythm. The wind whipped hard in the edges of his eyes, despite the goggles, and Greg had to shield his eyes from the sting.

"Do we have helmets on this thing?" yelled Greg over the din of the engine. "We could have been killed!"

"You have 418 troops looking for you, and you worry about dying in a road accident?" Wesley yelled back, his hair billowing crazily. "Get your priorities straight!"

Incense Master Sa Long stepped into the commune, his enforcers following close behind. He had insisted on handling this matter personally. As the son of the Dragon Head, second in command and Enforcer of the Labs, no one opposed him. The guards in the corridors knelt as he passed, and all voices hushed at his approach. They all knew his reputation throughout the city. To speak was to die, to be heard was to be silenced.

The past evening had been busy. Sa couldn't believe that an outsider could sneak his way inside, and give five of the guards at the checkpoint the slip. Those fucking bodohs that called themselves guards were now basking away in the stockades on the roof. Some UV light would do them some good.

They didn't find the interloping 25, despite a building-wide search. Sa hadn't considered it much of an issue. Everyone knew there were those who tried to make their way into The Mountain to carve out a living. Life out there was harsh, and here they had the Dragons to protect them. Besides, it was better not to get the Dragon Head involved. Sa knew how his father was—easily worked up over nothing. As far as he was concerned, it was business as usual. Just like illegal immigrants before The Storm.

Then he was awoken in the middle of the night. Moonshine and two hours of sleep didn't go hand-in-hand. A Blue Lantern had reported an intruder in the labs, despite the fact he had no reason to be fixing anything. Groggy and swearing, Sa had found part of the lab shot up, and the only reason the damage wasn't any worse than it could have been was that he had had all lab guards equipped with hollow-point ammunition, projectiles with hollow cavities in place of an otherwise sharp tip, which reduced penetration through hard surfaces. Some of the lab equipment were scheduled to run experiments for the last few weeks, but the power shutoff had brought them all back to square one. To make matters worse, with some of the testing equipment toast, and one of his best researchers missing, progress on Project Evermore would be delayed. He had questioned the Blue Lantern and felt something was up. He intended to find out what that was.

"So none of you saw anything strange?" he asked. Commune 11 gathered before him, all with their hands behind their heads. No one spoke. They all knew it wouldn't spare them. To get on with their lives was all they asked for.

The Blue Lantern, whom the men knew as Lantern, stood before the rest, his eyes nervous. Damn right he should be. What did he expect, a reward? It wasn't called loyalty if you were paid for it. Besides, it was real suspicious, having been in the right place at the right time. Especially at one in the morning.

"You know why you're here," spoke Sa. He didn't have to raise his voice; everyone heard him just fine.

Lantern looked confused. "The guys haven't seen anything. I've already checked with them."

"Do. Not. Test. Me," said Sa. His voice was silent and deadly, carrying malice and fury. "It was long past the time of your duties when you made your report. An outsider should not have gone unnoticed for so long in our domain. Which leads me to believe you had been harbouring him. Maybe even now."

"I would have reported him if so, Incense Master," replied Lantern. "I'm sure the others would too."

"Perhaps you grow weary of our hospitality?" asked Sa. "Perhaps you think your reward insufficient for a service so great? Or maybe a deal struck and unfulfilled?"

Lantern's eyes flickered, and Sa nodded, satisfied.

"It has been a shitty day for me, and yet I still find myself awoken at one in the fucking morning," continued Sa, his tattoos flexing as he paced. The 49ers behind him stared motionlessly. "But you would make it a lot better should you tell me everything you know about this intruder, along with his motivations. Do it now, or Commune 11 faces immediate extinction."

"So ruthless, Sa, yet so ineffective," spoke a voice. Sa and his men turned. Few had heard that voice, and even fewer had seen who it belonged to. As one, everyone in the commune, Incense Master, Red Pole, 49er or otherwise, dropped to their knees.

Flanked by guards in enclosed helmets and form-fitting ceramic armour, a slim figure strode in their midst, dressed in silk robes not unlike those worn by emperors, with numerous tiny dragons embroidered onto its surface. Its tailor would have said they totalled 418, but was long dead due to a flaw in the stitching. Despite long white hair and a beard that suggested wisdom and maturity, the newcomer's eyes were hard and unyielding.

"Dragon Head!" Sa said. His knees trembled as they pressed against the ground. "You honour us with your pres—"

"Spare me the crap," said Dragon Ho quietly, and a hush fell over once more. No one dared move, for the Dragon Head's words were life and death. The Head of the 418, de facto ruler of all that was. His personal guard, the Dragon's Teeth, also known as DT, fanned out among those gathered. Their gear and armour were designed in the pattern of red and black scales, such that one could almost mistake them for dragons themselves. And they might well be. Only the fiercest and most deadly made it into the Dragon Head's inner circle.

Incense Master Sa was silent as the 418 leader looked disdainfully at his feet, as if the dirt would crawl up and consume him. As one of the most senior-ranking 418 leaders, he had carried out much of Dragon Ho's bidding. When a knife went missing a while back, he had a whole commune put to the torch. Another commune was relocated to the ruins, so that the scorched surroundings reminded them of what awaited rulebreakers. A careless word could mean death, if Dragon Ho so wished it.

"Two years back, I was made aware of a mutiny in one of our Resource Centres," continued Dragon Ho. "As such, I had personally requested you to keep your eyes open for any who may seek to undo our efforts. Efforts to build our civilisation back to its rightful place. And yet,"— here, Dragon Ho tilted his head just the slightest bit—"you failed to stop a lone intruder from breeching our walls. An intruder who had hours to bide his time and strike at our very core. Explain."

Being in charge of overall security, Sa had thought he could keep that quiet. He'd deal with those snitches later. "I had a building-wide search performed, Dragon Head. We didn't find him."

"And you didn't consider it a problem." It wasn't a question.

"We figured he had already left by then," choked Sa. His throat was starting to tense up, and shivers ran down his spine. "I didn't see a need to put everyone on high alert."

"And yet an altercation took place," whispered Dragon Ho, pacing before the gathered people. "Not in our stores, armouries or markets, but in our very labs!" He shouted the last part, turning on Sa. "Do you know what the labs mean to us, Sa? It's not just valuable equipment that was destroyed, but a breach of our experimental security! All that could bring us to war with the Old Guard! Do you know what will happen if anyone outside The Mountain discovers what we are doing?"

Sa cowered under his leader's tirade. "I'll make it right, Dragon Head. I swear it as your son."

"You've done enough," replied his father. He drew his pistol and fired.

Sa didn't know he had died, his skull fragmenting too quickly for him to register. Dragon Ho surveyed the mess before him, even as a guard wiped the blood off his shoes. He made a big show of blowing the smoke off the barrel of his customised .44 Magnum pistol before pointing it at everyone around him, the red dot of his laser sight dancing across 49ers and civilians alike. They trembled as the beam made contact.

"Let all those gathered know that none will be spared should they prove incompetent!" announced Dragon Ho. "Not my 49ers, nor my Red Poles. Not even the flesh of my blood. Only the strong survive!" A jerk of his head, and Sa's corpse was dragged away. It would find good use as fertiliser in the hydroponic farms.

"The intruder had help from one of our own," said Dragon Ho emotionlessly. "I want all lab personnel, regardless of rank to be questioned of their involvement. Han?"

"Yes, Master Ho," said a Dragon Tooth. Red scales on the upper half of his armour signified his rank as a DT Squad leader.

"I also want this 25 brought to the negotiation room," said Dragon, his gaze falling on Lantern. "He will tell us everything he knows about our interloper, including all manner of facts about his entry."

"I have no secrets!" exclaimed Lantern. At a command, two of the DTs fell upon him with truncheons, his whimpers dying quickly into silence.

Dragon Ho turned to DT Commander Huo, whose armour bore blue scales interspersed with red. Once a Red Pole, he had been commander of the DT for three years. Like a few of the 418, across his skin was tattooed the known names of his victims, along with the dates of major skirmishes. He had run out of space, however, and rumour had it that he wrote the additional names down on the scales of his ceramic armour.

"Prepare the men for war," said Dragon Ho. "I want all combat-ready Red Poles in the discussion room an hour from now. Once the men move out, I want all wireless communications to and from The Mountain cut. Field communications remain as per normal."

Huo nodded, not showing his surprise. "May I ask why, my Master?"

"Something tells me the intruder may have gotten help from The Mountain. This shall end. And before I forget, execute the guys who shot up my labs."

BROKEN NATION

GREG NEVER EXPECTED to ride down one of the many highways in Singapore in a vehicle again. But then, there were so many things he hadn't expected less than two weeks ago.

For one, he could hardly imagine making his way back to the home city he had left so long ago. Second, he didn't expect to survive when pitted against what was now the most powerful force in Southeast Asia, or even the world. Whatever's left of it.

And thirdly, who, even in their wildest dreams, could fathom riding in the sidecar of a fully-working motorbike, teeth chattering away with a kid beside him, driven by a member of a delusional cult? Who himself betrayed no emotion as pothole after pothole was surmounted by the humming wheels of a refurbished bike? Which itself seemed capable of crumbling at one push of its brakes?

But Greg had never expected to be free of the mines. And that's saying something.

He recognised the stretch of highway they were now on, if it could be called that. For the first time in his life, Greg realised that despite the rusting hulks of what remained of roadside traffic, they hadn't experienced a single traffic jam. He found himself laughing at the incredulity of it all. He had escaped with his life intact from a ruthless triad and a wacky horde, only to concern himself with traffic conditions? What a true Singaporean he had proven to be.

With the noise the motorbike was making, he had to wonder if anyone was watching, though Greg figured they would be hard pressed to keep up. But then, he knew better than to underestimate the 418.

"You doing okay?" yelled Wesley across the din of the motor. Greg had to look around to confirm it was the cultist speaking to him.

"Do I have a choice?" replied Greg. Only now did he realise his fingers were numb from gripping the handlebar before him. Guo Li seemed to fare similarly, burping every now and then, but having known kids first-hand, Greg knew he wouldn't admit it.

"We could always stop for a break," shrugged Wesley. "But we're in unfamiliar territory, so I'll prefer it if we make it across the AYE, at least. It's been awhile since I've been through the area, and there's no telling who could be waiting for us. There're always bandits and scavengers to contend with."

Greg wondered if the roar of the motorbike hadn't already alerted the whole country to where they were. They had been on the road for the better part of forty minutes. In better times, they would have reached the city area by now, but broken roads and vehicle wreckages made traversing the roads a nightmare. The hard swerves and braking motions were all Greg could bear. He would rather be stuck in a broken-down MRT, if they still existed. But then, he wouldn't be getting anywhere.

"What were you doing so far out?" Greg asked. "Surely the scavenging is easier nearer to the Sanctum?"

"The Admin required more solid-state memory for the intranet servers. They could barely keep up with the bandwidth required by our growing flock. I went on several expeditions to find some," answered Wesley. He accorded Greg a grin. Of all the cultists, he was the most capable of human expression. But then, Wesley was a field operative.

"Where from? I thought the stores were all closed."

"Up ahead to the right is Keppel Harbour," replied Wesley, waving a hand towards the direction of the sea. Past the wind whipping in his eyes, Greg could see a field of shipping containers, waiting out their eternal vigil. Faded markings reminded all of the shipping empires that once existed, never to awaken again. Towering above the containers were the crooked skeletons of the cranes that handled them, a further reminder that nothing would ever be the same. Jin had once commented that the cranes looked much like four-legged dinosaurs, and now, they were. Long extinct and forgotten.

"Right after The Crash, or The Storm, as all you Offline call it, there was plenty of salvage here," explained Wesley. "The shipping staff and guards left quickly, and it didn't take long for other survivors to realise this was a one-stop source for whatever they needed. So many came here on a shopping trip, raiding what they could. Then the gangs came in and, well, you can imagine the bloodbath." Wesley shrugged.

"Most of the imported food and water's all gone now, but lots of stuff still remain," continued Wesley. "Stuff nobody likes to carry, like furniture and washing machines. But one of the containers had server cabinets bound for Singapore Polytechnic! Made by Sun Microsystems too. A bunch of them were fried, but salvageable. The Administrator saw it as a sign that we were blessed."

The bike veered suddenly, and for a moment, Greg thought Wesley had lost his concentration in the midst of his reminiscence. Then he saw it. A line of rusted road spikes, almost invisible in the years of dust on the road. The brakes of the bike screeched as Wesley spun the bike, and Guo Li let out a squeal. The vehicle jerked violently, and Greg felt himself thrown against the side of the sidecar.

Greg was amazed that the vehicle hadn't flipped over, but the sidecar had helped its balance immensely. Despite being dazed, he saw that the vehicle had stopped short against a concrete barrier.

He stumbled quickly over the edge of the sidecar, landing hard on the tarmac. Spotting a concrete barrier some metres away, Greg dashed towards it, vaulting across at the last moment. The top of the concrete barrier erupted into a cloud of fragments, followed by a loud report. Guo Li yelled from within the sidecar.

"Sniper!" yelled Greg, even as his heart froze. He had forgotten all about the kid in his haste, but he couldn't reach him now with a shooter out there.

"What's happening?" whimpered Guo Li. "Are people shooting at us?"

"Stay where you are!" yelled Greg. He changed his position behind the barrier before peering out. They were on a pretty bare stretch of the highway, with little in the way of cover save for the roadside railings, though there were gaping holes in places. He couldn't quite see where the shooter was coming from, though there were several candidates for a sniper's nest. A tall pile of shipping containers. A shipping crane with its legs bent at a precarious angle. Even a building in the distance, though it was much too far for a gun of this calibre. From the damage it had done on the concrete, it had to be firing .338 Lapua at the most, but more likely 7.62 NATO. But what worried Greg the most was not the unseen enemy, but those he could see. Alerted by the sniper, or perhaps by another lookout, a group of six survivors were dashing up the flyover exit towards where they were, wielding an assortment of weapons. Greg dropped back to cover in time to avoid the next shot.

"Greg, where're you at?" called a voice, and Greg heaved a sigh in relief. Wesley was still alive, at the very least.

"Keep your head down! There's a sniper about!" called Greg. "Have you found cover?"

"I'm crouched behind the bike. But that won't stop a well-placed 7.62. I estimate the shot came from your two o'clock! You got a visual?"

"Not on the sniper, but there are some thugs coming up towards us."

"Why am I not surprised. 418?"

"I can't tell. They don't seem like the type from The Mountain. No tattoos and guns," answered Greg. He chanced a look out. "Do you think you can get a shot at the sniper? I'm kind of pinned down. From the speed of sound, I'm guessing he's at maybe five hundred metres?"

"Too far. Our 5.56 rounds can't do shit at that range. We'll just be wasting ammo here."

"If only we have some smoke grenades," growled Greg. It was a simple enough tactic, when one had the right stuff. Pop some smoke into an area, and the sniper won't be able to see anyone to shoot at. But a brotherhood of code-worshippers wasn't exactly a well-stocked army, all things considered.

"Smoke ... " Wesley mused. "Greg, I need you to draw the sniper's fire!"

"The fuck do you mean?" yelled Greg as another shot smashed into the concrete behind him, hard enough to jar his back pressed against it. Yep, definitely 7.62 NATO. The sniper must have thought it would go right through. With .338 Lapua it would have. Greg didn't expect himself to panic—not here, not now, but already he could feel the symptoms. His hands shook as they gripped his glorified Nerf blaster, even as he wondered if he and the rest would ever make it out of this mess. It would be a fine thing if he survived the years in the mines, not to mention tangling with the 418, only to die from a shot delivered by some coward behind a scope. What was the point of it all? They were just two men against the unseen death.

Then Greg saw Guo Li's head sticking out, both fearful and curious. Some of the approaching survivors lifted what looked to be javelins and spears for a toss.

Greg yelled, dashing out from behind the barricade. Sliding himself bodily across rough, painful road, he aligned the makeshift sights of his gun and fired at the advancing force.

Two of the men went down at once, too shocked to even cry out. The rest scattered against the roadside partition and Greg rolled himself behind one. The sniper fired once more, though his shot went wide, scattering tarmac. Wesley could be heard fumbling with the motorbike, and Greg wondered if for all of his efforts, the cultist had decided to make a run for it.

With a gush, smoke erupted around the bike. Not the white smoke that pours out of a standard smoke grenade, or even a fumigating machine, but bright red smoke more akin to that used to mark a landing zone.

Or the smoke used by the RSAF for National Day Parades.

"Get your ass in the sidecar now!" came Wesley's voice. Greg shook himself out of his amazement. Already the smoke had spread out, given him a zone of safety he could run right through. He dashed towards the epicentre of the smoke screen, flinching slightly as the sniper fired wildly into the smoke. Wesley had taken the chance to drag the spike strip aside, flinging it to the side of the road.

"You doing okay, Guo Li?" asked Greg. The boy's eyes were wide as he looked about him, and Greg could only imagine how he felt, being surrounding by a fog the colour of blood, while gunshots erupted around him.

Wesley dashed back to the bike, and revved it. A survivor dashed towards the sidecar, brandishing a steel pole. Greg had no time to dodge even as the assailant swung it against his skull. A flash of stars erupted across his vision, and already the survivor grappled with him. The ex-soldier tried to fight him off, but his head was hurting too badly.

So he did the only thing he could. Gripping the barrel of his fallen AV-2, he clubbed the survivor on the head. Once. Twice. Even after his victim's hands grew limp, Greg didn't stop.

The bike finally sputtered and pulled out, still emitting smoke, and the survivor fell away. The remaining survivor screamed in fury, and Greg saw the look in Guo Li's eyes. Not disgust, but fear.

Wesley adjusted a knob, and the red smoke spewed at a 60-degree arc behind them, concealing them from shooters, and yet allowing them to see. Sure enough, not one more shot was fired upon them. Ammo was too precious these days.

There exists a saying that one must not become a monster while fighting them. Sadly, kids didn't understand just how harsh the real world was. Guo Li had refused to speak about what happened, shooting Greg angry looks every now and then. Greg was not worried—Guo Li was going to have to get over it, as long as the world remained this way.

Wesley had decided the coastal route was no longer safe; sooner or later, they would run out of smoke, which also acted as a beacon that signalled where they were. As Greg had guessed, the canister had been salvaged off a grounded fighter jet retrofitted for the Singapore Airshow. They passed through what was left of the Outram Park area, where the gaping eyes of ruined buildings stared forlornly, broken segments open in gaping screams. Greg kept his weapon at the ready, but no movement of any kind could be seen. Plastic bags and years of crap littered the street, and to his surprise, people still found the time to paint graffiti upon the cars and walls in the area. He supposed the old laws didn't matter anymore when there's no one to cane you.

Wesley stopped at the side of a street corner, his shoulders slumped. The sputter of the motorbike died down.

"Wesley?" Greg asked. As always, the guardian's eyes were covered by his goggles, making it hard to read his expression. But his shoulders and arms were shaking, as if by a great loss.

"The Sanctum's been silenced," whispered Wesley. "The voices that lead from it to us, now gone."

It took a moment for Greg to realise what the guardian was saying. "You lost contact with the Sanctum? Since when?"

"Right before we encountered the thugs on the highway. The 418 has found my brothers, I'm sure of it. Our faith can only do so much against tech and steel. I'll kill them all!" The yell reverberated around them, a faint echo bouncing off the surrounding buildings.

Greg had never seen Wesley in such a state. But then, he really didn't know much about the Brotherhood to begin with. But he knew they had communion with each other via digital means, plugged into the intranet that allowed their minds to meander with one another, closer in being than anyone could ever be. Besides, one could hardly deny the camaraderie members of a brotherhood had. As close as kinship, if not more so. To many of them, this was probably their only family. Before he had arrived, they lived in relative peace.

But now …

"How exactly are your communications broadcasted, Wes?" asked Greg.

"The hell do I know? N33r and ITm4ster set it all up," snapped Wesley. "Probably some form of 5G or radio transmission."

"If the signal is piggybacked onto the 418 comms frequency, the 418 may have cut it off Manually," explained Greg. "The Brotherhood might still be alive."

"But if they're not …" Wesley's voice rose to a growl.

"If they aren't, do you really think fighting in the name of vengeance is going to do anything for the cause?" asked Greg. "You'll still a member of the Brotherhood. Getting control of the Server is just the start; a beginning to further your Brotherhood's goals. Don't let's stop now."

Wesley raised an eyebrow, the one that could be seen above his goggles, anyway. "If I didn't know any better, I would say you were trying to further your own cause."

"Aren't we all? At least our goals are aligned in that aspect. And I'll say snatching the Server from the 418 is a pretty good opportunity for vengeance."

The distant sound of explosions could be heard, and the

three of them whipped their heads in that direction. It was coming in the direction of the old city.

Mortar fire? That can't be good. Wesley gave a huff and rode on.

As they neared the source of the ruckus, it was obvious that the explosions were part of a coordinated effort. From across the river, the three of them could see the city lit up sporadically by fiery blasts, the dust of old concrete fogging the air. Guo Li looked worried, and even Greg was starting to have a sense of foreboding about the whole thing. The explosions were loud enough that it jarred the very metal of the bike, and it was far too risky to drive the bike right into the city. Even with silenced engines, it would attract far too much attention.

"It seems they've let loose the dogs of war," said Wesley simply. "Sounds like 120mm HE shells too. These guys aren't messing around."

"They use dogs for war? I thought they got guns what?" said Guo Li, his brow wrinkled.

"He doesn't mean actual dogs. Wesley's quoting Shakespeare," explained Greg.

"Shakespeare's a dog?"

"Never mind," said Greg hurriedly. "Wesley, I think we'd better go on foot. The bike's gonna be an obvious target if we bring it in."

"N33r would be pissed," said Wesley. His voice carried no emotion.

"N33r would want you to stay alive. The bike's already done its job on the highway," reminded Greg. "It's nearing nightfall.

We have a better chance of making it through without it."

Wesley sat in silence for several moments. "Fine. Get out, the both of you."

Greg helped Guo Li out of the bike, and the two of them stood a respectful distance away. Wesley himself knelt before the bike, placing a hand upon the handlebars. He muttered a long string of syllables, of which Greg could assume was some kind of Codist mantra. It had high and low notes, and after a while, Greg realised Wesley was speaking in binary code.

"May The Cloud preserve you," finished Wesley, popping a switch. He made his way over to where Greg and Guo Li stood. The bike flashed bright white, so bright that Greg and Guo Li squealed, shielding their eyes. When the flames died down, all that was left of the bike was a steaming, melted mess. The acrid smell of burnt plastic and a chemical smell which Greg recognised as phosphorus hung in the air.

"His will was done," said Wesley dully, and Greg guessed he was either talking about N33r, or the bike that had brought them this far. "Let us continue, and speak no more of this."

Wesley hefted his carbine in his hands and strode off towards an underpass that led under a bridge that used to stand over the Singapore River. Beyond him, the skyline of the post-Storm city stood, framed by the ruins of the old city. Once, the buildings stretched out to the sky, competing for space where land cost several thousand dollars per square foot. Now they stood crooked and forgotten, billions if not trillions of dollars in real estate gone forever. Just like civilisation, and COE.

Greg turned to Guo Li, whose mouth was open in confusion.

"Best save your questions for later, kid."

As they got deeper into the city, the sound of mortars got louder, such that dust from the buildings regularly rained in a choking mess upon the three. Much of the city was levelled to piles of rubble that rivalled hills, with bent beams and cracked columns holding up what remained of it. Greg started to worry that the shockwaves caused by the mortar shells would pry loose a supporting beam, or worse, tip a building down upon them. But for all the dust and smaller bits of rubble that came loose, not once did anything larger tumble out of place. Compared to the effects of The Storm, the rumbling probably rated low in damage capability.

"What's going on here?" choked Greg as another cloud of dust settled. Wesley had passed around some old face masks people used long ago during the annual haze, but the dust was all- encompassing in its coverage. The swimming goggles they wore helped to prevent them from going blind, but quickly fogged up. It was already starting to get cold as night fell.

"I'm guessing your actions in the labs had a bigger impact than expected," said Wesley. "The 418 aren't just gun-toting tattoobacks; they've got stuff from the old SAF camps too."

"But what are the mortars targeting?" asked Greg. "Surely the 418 aren't expecting to level the whole city in the hope of getting us. It'll take far too much time and ammo for that."

"In all the time since I've been blessed by The Cloud, I've never been inside the Old City, only the outskirts," said Wesley. "It is said you can't get more than ten metres past the river without being stopped by the Old Guard. Have you noticed that we haven't been challenged so far? We've got to be at Raffles Place already. The Old Guard has their home somewhere around, and I'm pretty sure the shelling's to keep them busy. Something big's happening."

Sounds of gunfire could be heard around the corner of a road junction, followed by shouts and yells. They hunkered down against the collapsed roof of a bus stop, rifles at the ready. Several figures ran past about, 50 metres up ahead, rifles gripped tightly in their hands. They wore what looked to be an assortment of grey and dark-green pants, as well as running vests of different colours. Greg's eyes boggled. He had seen those clothes more often than most. Back before The Storm, each military formation had their own colour-coded running vests. It wasn't uncommon to see civilians using them out of camp, a souvenir of their enlisted days.

"Fall back! There's too many!" shouted one of the runners. Unlike the rest, who were equipped with no more than a rifle and waist pouch, this one wore his SBO, complete with helmet and LBV. He wore a full grey No. 4, the camouflaged combat dress of the Singapore Armed Forces, with its sleeves rolled, the dust and grime of the city greying it further.

One of the men crumpled, following a loud report of fire. The section IC turned to him in shock.

"This way!" The leader swung an arm towards where Greg, Wesley and Guo Li were hiding. "It's the safest way back to the City!"

"They're coming this way!" hissed Greg. "We got to move!"

Greg and Wesley made their way to the edge of the street, where they would be less noticeable. That was when all hell broke loose.

First, the ragtag assortment of a squad dashed down the street they were on, arms and legs a blur even as they escaped their pursuers. Their eyes widened in mingled anger and shock as they spotted the two interlopers, both dressed in a manner never seen before. Their leader yelled a warning, raising his rifle as he did.

Second, their pursuers appeared around the street corner. Two pickup trucks with retrofitted front grills and off-road tires, complete with fighters hanging off the siderails. Bare-chested and spotting red armbands, they were, without a doubt, 418 troopers. And they were packing heat, if the Ultimax 100s and GPMG were anything to go by.

Third, Guo Li tripped over and fell, his high-pitched squeal resonating in the otherwise quiet street.

Time seemed to freeze, so Greg did what he had been doing for the last six years: follow his instinct. Whipping the 25mm launcher from Wesley's hip holster, he raised it up and fired.

Compared to the more common 40mm grenade, the 25mm grenade was not as suited for use against vehicles, given its smaller payload. But it was not the weapon that matters so much as its target.

The engine of the first pickup erupted in flames, throwing its passengers all over the place. The second pickup behind it failed to stop in time, colliding in a mass of bent metal and glass. The uniformed leader and his squad looked from Greg to the chaos, and back again, confusion creasing their features.

"Another grenade!" yelled Greg, even as he disengaged the catch of the break open system. The spent casing of the 25mm remained stuck, and he fought vainly to rip it out.

"No time for that, fuckers coming in hot!" barked Wesley. "Fire for effect!"

Greg shoved the 25mm launcher into his own waistband. The passengers on the second pickup hadn't wasted any time. Despite their disorientation, they had started spreading out to whatever cover could be found. Some had let out bursts of fire as they did, sending Greg and Wesley ducking.

"Get back! We'll cover you!" yelled Greg to the uniformed

leader. He had no idea who this was, but any enemy of the 418 deserved a chance in his book. He raised his rifle to eye level, squeezing off his trigger. A 49er stumbled into another, both of them toppling. Greg yelled as an aimed shot shattered the concrete before his face, spraying it in choking dust. He would have gone blind without his goggles. He fell back into cover, and Wesley took over his spot. Without breaking cover, the Guardian stuck his carbine out above himself, squeezing off a volley of shots. Yells pierced the air.

"You weren't even aiming!" gasped Greg in surprise. "Practice much?"

Wesley looked disdainfully back at him. "GoPro camera. Provides real-time footage of weapon sights to my neural stream. Helps a ton with blind firing." Greg now knew why Wesley had gotten that weapon from N33r instead of him.

A loud squeal pierced the air. Greg chanced a look. One of the 49ers had gotten to Guo Li, and was snatching him up despite his fighting back. Greg aimed his AV-2, but knew it was hopeless. There was a big risk of hitting Guo Li in the process. A lousy caretaker he proved to be.

A blur dashed towards the 49er, descending upon him as he vaulted a block of concrete. It was the leader of the escaping squad. He swung an arm with almost martial proficiency against the thug. A flash of steel, and the 49er gurgled, clutching his neck. Keeping low, the squad leader threw Guo Li over a shoulder, dashing back towards where his men had fled.

"Come with us! There're more on the way," he barked to Greg and Wesley.

"And go where? This street's far too open!" Greg yelled back.

"Follow me if you want to live." The leader plodded on away from the fighting.

Greg fired off one more burst, before dashing after the leader, Wesley close behind. Seconds later, the cover they were at erupted in a cloud of dust and concrete shards, a 418 frag grenade having gone off. They ducked into a side alley of what had been one of many office buildings, now littered with piles upon piles of rubble. Another right turn, and they found themselves beside a collapsed building. Miraculously, a shorter building still stood, metal slats making up its walls. It took a moment for Greg's memory to recall what it was. One of the many air exhaust outlets for the underground MRT system, it was something the public walked by each time they commuted to school or work, never giving it much thought.

Only this time, the squad leader ran up to the door set in its side, fumbling with the lock.

"Get in, the two of you!" yelled the squad leader as the door popped open. "Jun Hao, set up a tripwire and claymore in the dust. The rest of you, fall in!"

Greg and Wesley squeezed through the door. Almost immediately, the echoes of the fight were softened, dull thuds resounding against the walls of the confined space. Greg could see this entrance had been used before; footprints in the dust showed that much. A large grill took up most of the floor, a great unmoving fan rotor beneath it. Beyond it, darkness loomed, darker than the darkest night. Several planks of wood lay against the wall. A hardhat still hung on its hook, with missing outlines showing tools that were missing. An electrical control box sat against the wall, dim and lifeless.

The rest of the squad bundled into the room. One of the guys threw the lock, slotting planks across the door handles. Greg saw that the door had been reinforced with sheets of metal, all haphazardly affixed to the surface. A loud boom erupted from the outside followed by screams, the claymore mine having done its deadly work.

"Get into the tunnel," ordered the squad leader. The grill across the fan was pulled away, revealing a ladder. Two soldiers went first, followed by Greg and Wesley. The click-clack of feet on ladder felt unfamiliar, strange even. Back on flat ground, they passed several more fans as they walked, their footsteps giving off an echo as they did. Guo Li was ushered along by the squad leader, his eyes wide as they walked.

"What were the 418 doing here?" asked Greg as they came into a wider tunnel. "We heard the explosions from afar."

Greg should have expected this, but he hadn't. As one, the soldiers stopped in their tracks, weapons raised towards him and Wesley. The squad leader's pistol found itself against Greg's neck, its coolness a reminder of the dangers throughout the wasteland.

"What?" Greg spluttered as he found himself relieved of his weapon, his arms held behind him. Wesley was struck from behind and held likewise. Aside from a cough, he didn't make any other noise.

"Did you really think you could infiltrate our home so easily?" demanded the squad leader. Now that he was up close, Greg saw that he had an epaulette affixed to his vest, three horizontal bars identifying him as a military Captain. A name patch stated his name as Ping SH. "Search these two," he ordered his men.

"You're jumping to conclusions, Captain," growled Greg, two of the men patting him down. "If you wanted to know who we are, just ask. There's no need for this high-handed fuckshit."

"Really?" asked Captain Ping, his brow stretched in a sneer. "You seem pretty well-armed compared to the average wastelander." He held up the AV-2 Greg had carried. "Granted, it looks like a toy, but its ammunition is not." The Captain ripped out its magazine, exposing the discoloured cartridges at the top.

"The wasteland is an unforgiving place. These are but our means of defence," said Greg. "Whoever travels unarmed is a fool."

"And whoever bears guns has the means. The means to make or steal them," said Captain Ping, and Greg knew he had seen through them. "418 spies, perhaps? What bidding do you do for your masters?"

"We come not to enforce the will of the 418, but to fight against them," said Greg. "A task that cannot happen while you hold us here."

"Next time, we let these guys die," snorted Wesley. Someone had removed his goggles, revealing a pair of angry eyes. "Bunch of ungrateful shits."

The rest of the men exhibited a mix of annoyance and uncertainty. Now that they weren't under fire, Greg saw they wore a haphazard mix of gear. All wore the military formation running vests he had seen earlier. He recognised the green digital camouflage pants a couple wore as that of the Singapore Army. Another two wore the grey digital camouflage pants of the Navy, which wasn't altogether common, but had greater camouflage capabilities in urban areas. All wore waist pouches stocked with ammunition, except for one who wore the 1st-Gen "Bra-Strap" load bearing vest. They held a mix of SAR 21s and M16s, but no other support weapons.

"You guys are part of the Old Guard," said Greg in realisation.

Captain Ping leaned back, eyebrows raised. "Tell me something I don't know." He didn't lower his gun.

"Pardon me, but the ragtag appearance of your gang— your squad made me think you were just a bunch of survivors making do. I thought the Old Guard defended the City and all around it. Not retreat before a bunch of glorified thugs."

"That's because the 418 had never come in full force!" yelled the Captain. "They may have sent small patrols every now and then, but they know there's nothing for them here. Yet, less than an hour before your arrival, the 418 arrived, not in mere scout patrols, but full combat companies! Before that, they had never once pushed into the Old City. Just as my men and I were caught in the fray, who should turn up but the both of you! Most convenient indeed."

"Convenience doesn't explain it," denied Greg.

"Then what're you doing here? Who do you serve?"

"That's not for you to know. But we're on your side."

Captain Ping gripped his P228 pistol harder, looking for a moment he would use it. But one of his men spoke.

"Sir, perhaps we should bring them to the Colonel," suggested the soldier. He wore the red and yellow vest of the Headquarters 9th Division, Infantry, with a 3SG epaulette on his ILBV. He looked just about old enough to have been enlisted before The Storm began. "They might have some insight on what's going on."

"And what, Ang? Lead foes to our home?" snorted the Captain.

"Regardless of hostility, they did save our lives," said Sergeant Ang, and the other soldiers looked uncomfortably back at each other. "Besides, it's clear they aren't ordinary wastelanders, judging by their equipment. If they have intel on the enemy, the Colonel needs to know about it."

"Fine!" The Captain threw up his arms. Greg flinched. "But if any of these guys run, they're dead."

THE CITY BELOW

GREG SAW MORE OF the MRT infrastructure then he had ever had in his entire life. But then, it wasn't like they had tours to sign up for even back in the day.

The tunnels lead past several collapsed areas, including what appeared to have been temporary living spaces at some point. Otherwise-empty rooms showed an excess of empty food and drink packets, the sharp smell of long-rotten food or dead rats piercing the air. Many a smashed door and skeleton told its own story of what had happened. Greg saw calendars flipped permanently to 15th February, a reminder of the day it all happened.

Eventually, the maintenance tunnels led out to one of the main MRT train tunnels. Even before The Storm, most people, rich or poor, had to depend on the MRT at some point. And now, after The Storm, he had to travel its tunnels not once, but twice, just to get where he needed! Greg almost laughed out loud at the dark humour of it.

"Are there any Mindless here?" Greg couldn't help but ask. He hadn't expected anyone to understand what he meant, but their actions said it all. Some of the soldiers tightened their grip on their rifles, with one muttering a prayer under his breath. The Captain glanced at him, while Wesley remained impassive as always.

"There used to be, but we cleared most of the nearby areas some time back," replied Ang. "Ammo was short, so we had to drive them away and isolate part of the train network with barricades. Every now and then, one would somehow find its way in, but that's what our patrols are for. You encountered them? Where exactly?"

"Somewhere between Botanical Gardens and one-north station. There's got to be at least fifteen of them in that stretch," replied Greg.

Captain Ping frowned. "Are you going to sit down and have kopi and teh-si with this guy, Ang? If not, be quiet!" The journey onwards was spent in silence. The clop of boots and shoes echoed throughout the tunnel, dim beams of light doing little to pierce the circle of darkness.

They neared a collection of dim lights in the distance, which turned out to be a guard post. Of the six guards, two of them were asleep against the makeshift concrete barricade. The other four were seated on plastic crates much the same way as one would at the tables of a HDB void deck. No GPMG or support weapons were to be seen, with the only armaments being a couple of dull-coloured M16s which had been repainted countless times with Kiwi boot polish. By the look of the barrel grips, they weren't even 2nd-gen models, and were similar to those used by reservists during In-Camp Training. The old-generation M16s were, in Greg and many soldiers' opinions, pieces of shit. Their direct- impingement gas operated systems meant it fouled and jammed frequently, as the Americans learnt during the Vietnam War. Why anybody even kept them in stock was anybody's guess.

"Waaassup, Sir!" greeted a guard. His chevrons indicated him as a staff sergeant, and Greg wondered at the state of the Old Guard to not accord their officers the necessary respect.

"Guard Duty is relak time also?" scowled the Captain. The staff sergeant shrugged as his men laughed.

"Nobody come this way, not like anything will happen!" drawled the staff sergeant.

"We just got back from a war zone, so you better do your damn jobs!" snapped the Captain.

"When the enemy comes, you better not be so relak or bochup! You mati then you know!"

The staff sergeant nodded, but as the squad passed, Greg could see the derision in his eyes. An army survives on its people and morale. He shuddered to wonder what the other men would be like.

A couple of makeshift steps of concrete blocks led from the tracks to the platform, and here, Greg could see that an entire city lay beneath the old one.

Although the station's signboards had long been dismantled for materials and parts, Greg recognised the layout as that of City Hall station. Tents and shacks of plywood and plastic sheeting took up much of the platform space, with scruffy-looking people going about their lives. Cooking fires glowed here and there, with the occasional clink of ladles against metal. Someone had lit a flame beneath an old escalator step, grilling an assortment of items on the ridged surface. Against the wall at the far corner was what looked to be a vegetable garden of sorts, with fluorescent lighting providing a little of the light the plants needed. As an interchange station, City Hall compromised of several different levels, each serving a different line when train services still existed. As they were led up a rickety escalator which had had its steps replaced by wood panelling, Greg and Wesley could see the level that had serviced the North-East Line was now a dedicated work floor of some kind. Bits of scrap and rubble from the topside were disassembled by teams, with the constant sound of hammering and sawing permeating the air. Different metal parts such as rebar and screws were sorted to different workbenches, where other crew worked on repairs. There was even what appeared to be a reloading bench, with a civilian sorting out different ammo casings from a pile while another ground gunpowder ingredients with a mortar and pestle.

At what used to be the station control centre, the Captain stopped. "Lau, I need to speak to Colonel Beng," he said to the guard within. The guard looked up from a worn Jeffery Archer paperback.

"Colonel Beng is busy in the Duty Room. Is there any particular reason?" said the bored-looking lieutenant. Just like in the Army of old, he wore a tag on that identified him as the day's Duty Officer. Despite the booms that could be heard topside, the underground city wasn't the hive of activity Greg had expected. There were armed fighters shuttling here and there, but none looked too panicked or even in a hurry. He could see that Wesley had noticed this too, his normally stoic expression now creased in a frown. If this was how things were like in times of distress, Greg shuddered to think what it was like in better times.

"We've brought in two tangos in need of questioning, and one child in need of medical attention," said the Captain. "I need to give the Colonel an urgent sitrep."

"We have a procedure for that. Follow it," said Lau. "Holding Cell's where you last saw it." He turned back to his book.

Captain Ping stepped up to the door set beside the booth, and yanked it open. Pulling the lieutenant from the chair, he slammed him forcefully against a filing cabinet, scattering what appeared to be a pile of reading material, including old sports magazines.

"I may tolerate your shit during peacetime, you bloody cheebai kia, but we are in a state of potential war!" roared Captain Ping. "So get off your ka cheng and do your fucking job! Inform the Colonel that this is an emergency!"

The lieutenant threw a punch into the Captain's midriff, something unheard of during Greg's stint in the Army. Captain Ping grunted, but before the lieutenant could reach for his sidearm, Sergeant Ang barged into the booth, jamming his SAR 21 into his chest. The rest of his men held their rifles uncertainly. None of the passing soldiers seemed to find that strange.

"I can shoot you now for assaulting my superior," hissed Sergeant Ang. "But we don't want blood all over the place, right? Not good for the next Duty Officer. Call Colonel now." He backed away slightly, as Captain Ping recovered.

Lieutenant Lau looked like he would gladly take on all of them, but instead reached for a switchboard. He pressed a red button labelled "COMMANDER" and spoke.

"Royal Guard, Captain Ping is cleared for entry," said Lieutenant Lau sullenly. "A status report awaits you."

"Roger that," said the radio. Captain Ping gave the lieutenant a glare before leaving.

"Put these two in the negotiation room," he told Sergeant Ang. "And get the kid to the medical bay."

"I want to talk to Uncle Kim Shang!" said Guo Li suddenly. The squad turned to look at him curiously.

"What do you know about Major Kim Shang?" demanded Captain Ping.

"He is my uncle. I used to live here also."

Greg turned to the kid. "You chose only now to tell us this?"

"I didn't know who these soldier guys were. Many come and go," said Guo Li. He had fallen into a sulk, the way Jin did whenever he wished to make a point. "Also, the uniforms you all wear, I don't know whether real or stolen."

Captain Ping gave an exasperated growl. "I can't just call anyone you like. The Major is a busy man."

"If you want do the right thing, then call him."

"Fine! I'll go get the Major too. See to these guys," said Captain Ping to his men. "And no talking to anyone about what's happening up there! Not until me and the officers hold a briefing about it." Six men including Sergeant Ang marched Greg and Wesley away, while the rest took Guo Li away. The kid looked back at them, and Greg waved back reassuringly.

They now walked through what Greg—and most likely Wesley—remembered as the station's entrance to what had been Citylink. A labyrinth of underground malls with entrances interspersed all over the city, what used to be a total of four escalators leading up to Raffles City mall were now collapsed in. Probably a good thing, because the booms from the city could still be heard, dust rumbling from the pile of rubble. Greg could only imagine what was going on above. Shelling, of course, but perhaps also troop movements and the like. He didn't know how numerous the 418 fighters were, but if the size of the army that had enslaved him and his family were any indication, there had to be thousands at least.

It was funny, really. Back before The Storm, the Government was always lamenting how few citizens wanted to enlist as a career soldier in the Armed Forces. There were less than 80,000 soldiers at any one time, more than half of which were conscripts. All these protected close to six million people. In the 21st century, such a size for an Army wasn't considered adequate.

Now, with the state of the world as it is, only a few thousand—a strength of several battalions—might be enough to defeat what was left of the Army, if you could call it that. Greg spied several squads dashing past, and in their eyes and slumped shoulders he could see their exhaustion. He wondered if they had any chance of holding out for just one day. In the open doors of what were once shops were a combination of medical bays and sleeping areas. A restaurant and several eateries had been converted to a mix of cooking areas and what appeared to be food and water storage.

They passed what used to be a large gym, with two guards in front. The glass storefronts still remained, stained and cracked in places, though several shelves with mesh nailed to it made up its perimeter fencing. Greg could see several uniformed soldiers within it, one of them gesticulating wildly as he yelled. The neatly-worn No. 4 uniforms, complete with sleeves folded to "Smart 4" seemed almost out of place in what could be best described as a chaotic setting. There were no computers or laptops, but large charts took up a whiteboard placed at the front of the room. What appeared to be an OHP projector displayed a transparent, hand-drawn map of a location. From the orderly rows of buildings and straight roads, it was most likely the city area. Several markings had been crossed out in red, with a green circle located in the centre. A smudged number indicated there were currently 24 troops in "Outdoor Ops".

"Don't tell me you have wounded men!" yelled one of the

soldiers who was slightly shorter than the rest, with white hair. "We still need eyes on the enemy. Going blind is the worst mistake we can make at this point in time."

"Colonel, the best chance we have is making sure the community is safe," said an officer. "We have enough food and water for another two weeks—"

"That shit won't do any good if the enemy attacks!" the Colonel spat back. At that moment, a door to the right of the room opened, revealing Captain Ping. However, Greg could see and hear no more as his group passed. Sergeant Ang lead them to another room where two guards sat playing a board game, the Singapore version of Monopoly. Greg smiled grimly at the disparity between the game of property ownership and the reality of the wasteland, where one never truly owned a home—you simply held onto it as long as you could. Just like this underground city.

"Yo, Min. I need to have two guys brought inside the Negotiation Room," said Sergeant Ang.

The guard tapped on a book labelled "Sign-In/Sign-Out". "Fill in the book and sign. Don't sign on the line, okay?" He gave Greg and Wesley a glance. "What, these two never do guard duty ah?"

"Err, no," said one of the squad members. "They are from the—"

"—the EW platform," finished Sergeant Ang quickly, glaring at the soldier. Greg saw him write "Sleeping on Duty" in the column labelled "Reason for Detainment".

"Oh okay." The soldiers went back to their game. "Any idea what's going on topside?" asked Min, almost like an afterthought. "Those bombings have been going on for some time now."

"Can't say anything about it. Captain's orders," said Sergeant Ang as he unlocked the door to a room beyond. Greg and Wesley walked inside. Bare walls and rectangular markings on the floor suggested this had been a maintenance area. Aside from six plastic chairs, and a couple more stacked in the corner, the room was devoid of furnishings. Sergeant Ang gestured towards the chairs.

"Sit here and wait. Follow any instructions the guards give you," he said before leaving. The door closed, leaving Greg and Wesley in silence.

"Well, so much for an uneventful trip," muttered Greg. "You doing okay, Wes?"

"As fine as I could ever be," came the reply. Without his goggles and helmet, the cultist looked bare and unguarded. The Old Guard had confiscated whatever they had, including their pouches. There was no way they were going to escape, not unless they considered fighting the guards. And even if they succeeded, there were more in the corridors.

"Any word from the Brotherhood?" asked Greg. The cultist wasn't much of a talker to start with, but something about his mood and demeanour suggested a deeper problem.

"No," said Wesley. "I could try boosting my reception, but those dicks took my power bank."

"I'm sorry?" The last time Greg had heard of a power bank being used was before The Storm. Now, of course, such things were moot. Did Wesley have a working radio with him?

Wesley tapped the back of his head. "For my neural interface. It normally uses my own body's electrical pulses, but it's only sufficient for default operating states. Reception above ground was fine, but this deep underground, more power is required to even get a signal."

Greg looked back at him. "There's so much I don't know about you and your c— your Brotherhood," he said. Close call, there.

"That's our point, isn't it?" said Wesley dryly.

"No, I meant—"

The door banged open, and several uniformed figures strode in. Greg and Wesley stood up immediately, only to find themselves at gunpoint. SAR 21-point to be accurate.

"I don't have time for this. Just who the hell are you two?" demanded Colonel Beng. Up close, Greg could see it wasn't just the hair on his head that was white—so was the stubble on his chin. The Colonel's bodyguards stood before them, levelling their rifles at the outsiders. Upon their arms were the black armbands of the Military Police. Although the No. 4 uniform the Colonel wore was familiar during Greg's time in the Army, the pistol and parang on his belt weren't.

Greg realised that for all he had been through these past few days, he really didn't have a good answer for that. Part of his mission didn't factor in having to explain himself along the way. What could he say? That he was an ex-slave who escaped, making his way back to save his son from being neutrally exploited with technology that may or may not exist? That accompanying him was a devotee of what many would describe as a whack-job cult, of which there was no telling what their ultimate aims in life were? But if he was to be shot, he would rather die having explained himself.

"My friend and I are headed to Gardens by the Bay." Even as the words left his mouth, Greg realised how stupid this sounded. "I'm trying to save my son," he added.

"Really? And yet, fire and death rain down upon us as we speak!" yelled the Colonel. "Do you expect me to believe that your timely arrival is a damn coincidence? What is the Dragon Head up to? Tell me now!"

"Let us explain—" began Greg, but at a jerk of the Colonel's head, one of the soldiers grabbed him by the arm, throwing him to his knees. The other swung the butt of his rifle against his head, and pain beyond imagination exploded across Greg's vision. The Colonel was yelling again, but Greg could barely hear it beyond the ringing in his ears. Wesley was now beside him, subjected to the same bullshit. He shuddered to imagine what the blows were doing to the cultist's digital implants.

"Colonel, I think we need to follow due process," said a voice. Greg barely recognised it as Captain Ping. "These two saved my men—"

"Triad scum are one and the same. They seek only to infiltrate our home, slinking in like the snakes they are!" The Colonel was positively spitting now. "I ask again: what are your Dragon Head's plans? Tell me now!" A kick of his boot sent Greg sprawling, only to be yanked upright again.

They called this a Negotiation Room. But now Greg knew its true purpose was interrogation. He couldn't even speak, with the blows upon him relentless. He realised that he would likely die here, unable to save Jin. It didn't matter how close he was, how hard he tried. What mattered was that at least Guo Li made it …

Guo Li. If they didn't bring him to his uncle as promised … Greg's head slumped, barely feeling the thuds upon him.

Getting injured or sick in the wasteland was dangerous. You never knew if a drug you needed still existed, or even if it did, was too expensive or dangerous to obtain. Being wounded was no different; not being able to run or fight greatly reduced your chances of survival, and there weren't any medical equipment to assess how bad it was. There was also the risk of the wound getting infected, which lead back to the first point.

Greg was therefore surprised when he woke. His eyes blinked hard as he tried to figure out where he was. Not the glorified Negotiation Room, that's for sure. It was dark where he lay, but there was no mistaking those straight silhouettes.

He was in a cell. He had gone from a slave camp to a prison.

Greg jerked upright, realising that he felt several points of a cold sensation in his wrist. Turning slowly, he could see Wesley had a hand closed around it, sitting perfectly still in the cell next to him. Greg only then realised that in the short time he had known Wesley, he had never seen the acolyte, or any of his brothers display much emotion. Now, despite all the bruises and cuts upon his face and arms, Wesley's face was creasing at certain intervals. One would think that Greg was on his deathbed.

"I'm okay, Wesley," said Greg. He made to pull his wrist away.

"Stay still! You still need calibration!" The acolyte hissed, gripping harder. It took Greg a moment to understand what he meant. Cool fingers. Calibration. His awakening, despite having been beaten close to shit.

He had been healed in a similar way back in the Sanctum. Wesley was doing it now, transferring or modifying electrical body signals through some sort of skin implant.

"What happened?" asked Greg. There didn't appear to be anyone else in the cell block, or even a guard. They were probably in a room outside, with enough light to play cards or monopoly or whatever unmotivated soldiers did. So much for the Eight Core Values of the SAF.

Wesley cast a lidded eye at him. "You seriously asking? Colonel Asshole and his guys beat the shit out of you. I manage to give a semblance of unconsciousness as they did the same to me. From my real-time recordings, they are putting us here until they have time to question us again. Captain Dickless was of no help."

"His life's on the line too," reminded Greg. "His leader seemed rather … unbalanced?"

"Just call him a cunt already," said Wesley, sounding irritated. "Based on my statistical analysis, someone dear to him had been victim to the 418, giving rise to his flights of fancy. The Cappy should still have done something, even if it was just to suggest they stick to the issue at hand. This whole mission just took a turn for the worse."

The two of them fell silent, the only sounds being their slow breaths.

"I never expected to be caught again," muttered Greg. He didn't like talking about his past, but it just felt right. "First the mines, now this. Well, you and your Admin held me for a while, but that probably doesn't count."

"Do you regret it?" asked Wesley. They both knew what he meant.

"Helping the Brotherhood? No. Jin's all I've left. You know that before the crap in the world started falling apart and shorting out, he wanted to be a programmer? At six, he was already looking through source codes in different Android phones." For the first time since he could remember, Greg chuckled.

"According to the Brotherhood, that makes him one of the Chosen Ones," said Wesley, his fingers twitching as Greg's frown returned. It struck him then, that rather than saying "my Brotherhood", the acolyte had described it in the third person.

"Perhaps," Greg shrugged. "What were you before all this, Wes? A hacker with the Anonymous Group?" He grinned.

Wesley accorded a smile that looked almost forced. "No. I was too busy countering threats both digital and tangible. Not all of 9th Signal Battalion's the bunch of slackers you imagine. Though I doubt there were any Edward Snowdens here."

"I didn't say—"

"You don't have to," said Wesley. "We all join the Army for a reason. What would yours be?"

"To ensure the SAF's equipment are up to date. To improve our technological and operational capabilities," said Greg. "I always believed technology made a big difference in whether we win or lose. It's the way of the world."

"Touché," said Wesley, looking about them. "You know what I mean."

"I signed on to the Army as a Computer and Signal Specialist with the Cyber Defence Group, because I wanted to play my part," said Wesley. "The way I saw it, we may fight with guns and explosives one year, and utilise cyber warfare the next. I liked my job, and did it well too. So the CDG eventually transferred me to 9th Signal Battalion where I protected the networks of the east of Singapore."

Greg tilted his head. "So what happened?"

Nobody needed to say he was asking about what Wesley did during The Storm. "I was lost. I was on duty securing our Information Grid, when everything just switched off. Our phones don't work, our comms got fried, and I could see everything we built descending into chaos. I was one of the few who knew where our critical server systems were located. Most of the guys had already left for their families and elsewhere. I figured that if I let the last of the information caches die, we go back to the Stone Age."

"I don't understand."

"Let me put it this way." Wesley mused for a second. "Mankind is constantly evolving, not so much in our physical respects, but in terms of technology and how we overcome problems. Now, the advancement of different civilisations is also primarily due to their superiority in warfare, which in turn is helped by technology. Steel weapons instead of stone. Guns instead of swords. For all of our dependence on modern electronics, there are barely any paper records of mankind's greatest achievements. The Storm had blasted us all back to the past, with practically all computers rendered inoperable.

"So I figured, that in order for us to come out of the past, I had to preserve what was left of it. And so I travelled to the known sites of the military and governmental servers. Each time I couldn't access it or the data was irrecoverable. When I went to Server 42 at Fusionopolis, that was when I found a greater impetus for my cause."

"You found the Brotherhood?" Greg could feel the aches and pains over him fading.

Psychological effect or not, Wesley's tech was working.

"Yep," nodded Wesley. "By then, the 418 had already taken over the building, and my SAR 21A was long out of ammo. I broke in through a hatch to the basement, figuring I could at least find a server system and download the recovery file to my portable hard disks. Little did I realise I had stumbled into the domain of the Brotherhood."

"They can't have been too happy to have a soldier find them," Greg muttered.

"The Brothers weren't but the Administrator saw it as a sign. He believed I had found them based on an encrypted signal they broadcasted, despite the fact it was purely by chance. My knowledge of programming languages convinced him further that I was to be their Guardian. They had a working server, even though it did little more than house Fusionopolis' databases, as well as what made up their intranet. By then, the 418 had set up their own power plant, and the Brotherhood only needed a meagre amount of power for their own uses. Server 42 had fifty percent of its data still intact, so I did what I could to make it work. Those admin codes I had helped.

"You have to understand that I could find no working computer or data reader until that point, and it seemed much like divine providence when I did. I may not have found the cache to the world's knowledge, but Server 42, and Fusionopolis, were enough for me then. My search was not in vain, and for a time, I was satisfied with Communion through the intranet, as well as my scavenger runs. The Brotherhood was thankful for the extra data and storage Server 42 provided, and I was more than welcome among them. The 3D drawings and simulations stored inside helped us construct our own devices, including some of N33r's designs. The Admin always told me that I would find greater purpose one day."

"So when you guys heard of the server at Gardens by the Bay ..."

"We knew it was time. I am the Brotherhood's crusader on this holy quest." Wesley let go of Greg. "How do you feel now?"

Greg flexed his arms, his fingers opening and closing. He felt good, considering he had been beaten ruthlessly for knowledge he didn't have.

"I feel good." Now that Wesley wasn't gripping him, he could see circuitry on where Wesley's fingerprints had been. "You were saying that you need a power bank for your systems? How much energy did you just use?"

"Only a little," replied Wesley drily. "This isn't a healing spell or anything like that. Adjusting the body's electrical impulses doesn't take much out of me."

"Forgive me for asking, Wesley," said Greg. Wesley stiffened. "But I would like to know why you had yourself …" Greg gestured to the back of his head, searching for the word. "… I don't know, modified?"

To Greg's surprise, Wesley smiled. "And here I was wondering when we were going to have this heart-to-heart talk."

"I meant no offense—"

"None taken. It's not like we have much to do anyway, unless someone actually frees us." Wesley leaned against the wall of his cell. "About the process you meant, you were asking how we of the Brotherhood have electronics placed inside us? We call it The Implantation. Only a qualified surgeon with knowledge of electronics is allowed to perform the operation. I had mine done after half a year with the Brotherhood. The way I saw it, the world shouldn't remain backward simply because most of it is gone. We have to adapt, and even evolve to meet changes. In order to prepare for the return of the Digital Age, or Reawakening, these implants will allow The Cloud to sense our devotion. It also allows us calculate the parameters of the mundane world, such as danger probability, along with many other variables. Living in the past doesn't do any good. Living in the future does."

The two of them were silent after that. Even the sound of bombing up top ceased. "I wonder what's happening to Guo Li," Greg finally said.

"He'll be fine. If anything, the Old Guard have more to worry about. Reminds me of a little cousin of mine. The way things turned out, that brat could have gotten away with murder and kidnapping," Wesley paused. "On hindsight, I wouldn't put it past the kiddo to forget all about us."

"He wouldn't."

"It is clear you have never experienced life in primary school."

"Did too! And it's a neighbourhood school!"

"From my experience, kids rarely think of the bigger picture. Immediate needs tend to nullify everything else," snorted Wesley. "He's probably scoffing whatever passes off as food in this dump, happy to be out of the wind and sun, while the two of us rot away in what's likely a forgotten corner of this place. Did you even hear any guards out there?"

"Did your neural implants tell you all that?" Greg couldn't help but be angry at Wesley's words. "Or did whatever functions as your search engine do that?" Guo Li had to have gone for help. He couldn't have left them.

"Hey, have some respect for other religions—" began Wesley, but at that moment, the lights to the cell turned on, blinding them both. Greg threw up his arms, in part to shield his face, and from any blows that may be coming.

"Sorry about the lights. Are the two of you Wesley and Greg?" a voice asked.

Greg briefly wondered why the soldiers would ask such a question, if they had been the one that threw him and Wesley inside in the first place. Then he realised that he had never told the Colonel or any of the soldiers their names.

"I'm Greg," he said, lowering his arm. "Guess who's Wesley." Before him, framed at the door he was slowly closing, stood a man about 1.8 metres tall and in his forties, though differing conditions of the post-Storm world could do a lot to change one's appearance. Unlike most of the soldiers previously seen, he wore a pair of grey cargo pants and a grey t-shirt. To any other person, he would have looked just like any ordinary guy. But to anyone who had worked with the Army, he was a senior soldier through-and-through. It was hard to explain how one knew: a mix of the person's gait and posture, coupled with either a confident or no-nonsense expression. He held a stack of something under an arm.

"A smartmouth. Guo Li must have forgotten to mention that," said the newcomer. His expression remained stoic.

"Sorry," said Greg. "Who may you be?"

"My name is Major Kim Shang," said the newcomer, and the two prisoners straightened at this. "You may also call me Major Shang. Guo Li told me of how the both of you rescued him from captivity, and brought him home. It will come of no surprise that I find it hard to believe this was your reason for coming here."

"We didn't expect to have to save Cap Ping and his men either," put in Wesley. "They put us behind schedule, if you must know."

Major Shang nodded. "Of course. Would that schedule involve heading to Gardens by the Bay? I for one am rather confused by what Guo Li was saying about what's going on there. He says the 418 had him held in a lab of some kind, and you found him?"

"The 418 are doing IT experiments on kids, Major," said Greg, standing upright. The Major looked surprised, but remained still. "One of those kids includes my son. Guo Li saw him. They're using the minds of kids to unlock a server of some kind, I don't know what. With that data, they could become the most powerful force in the wasteland."

Major Shang stared. He sounded doubtful when he next spoke.

"What you're saying belongs to the realm of science fiction," he said, eyes narrowed in what could only be annoyance. "Guo Li had also told me the both of you are part of a fanatical cult, who believes in the worship of computer systems. Your faith may be your anchor, but it does not make fact."

"I'm not from that cult. This guy is. And it's called a Brotherhood," said Greg. Wesley looked miffed. "Besides, they were monitoring the activities of the 418. Why do you think the 418 is attacking? Because they know someone is getting close in finding out about their plans. They had to make sure their only opposition, the Old Guard, is taken care of. What more proof do you need?"

A distant boom resounded in the distance. Yells could be heard in the corridor outside. The Major looked torn trying to come to a decision, then turned back to the two of them.

"Put on these uniforms," he said. "You're going to need them."

ONWARD AND FORWARD

It had been a long time since Greg or Wesley had worn a military uniform. But there was something reassuring about the light fabric against the skin, the way it seemed to lend meaning to whatever they did. For a certain few, that was why they put it on day after day.

The check-in area of the cell was deserted. If the situation had gotten worse since they arrived, the Old Guard was going to need all hands on deck, unmotivated or not. Greg couldn't help but notice both the name tags on his and Wesley's uniforms had the initials WONG KS, but he supposed the Major didn't have time and resources to put together something different. Major Shang had ordered Greg and Wesley to carry crumbling cardboard boxes with packets of something, in a bid to make them look less suspicious. Nobody did more than glance at them, however, so Greg supposed it counted for something. They were in a section different from where they had been interrogated, and it was all Greg could do to not lose sight of the Major, as civilians and soldiers were continually running past and potentially cutting them off. He kept hearing a PA announcement throughout the halls, but it was too convoluted to make out. Probably an activation order of some sort.

Major Shang unlocked the numerical lock of a door set into the side of a hallway, and entered. At first glance, it appeared to be a briefing room of some sort, with a table and chairs fronted by a large piece of cardboard with writing upon it. By the arrows and scribbles, Greg knew they were troop movement plans. Against the wall were a couple of red steel mesh cupboards, with the unmistakable shapes of guns and vests within it. Seated on the chairs were six other soldiers, including two Greg recognised—Captain Ping and Sergeant Ang sat near the head of the table. All of their equipment were either on the ground or placed at the side. No one saluted, so Greg assumed all unnecessary traditions had long since been dropped.

"Put that shit down anywhere." Major Shang gestured at the boxes. Greg and Wesley dropped them.

"These are the ones Guo Li mentioned," said Major Shang to those seated. Greg and Wesley nodded to them. "What I tell all of you gathered is highly classified, and not to be mentioned to anyone else. About a year ago, two of our scouts reported a convoy of vehicles travelling towards the direction of Marina Bay. Not the patrol units the 418 use for small-time raids, but covered lorries with an escort. By the time the news got back to the Colonel, they were nowhere to be found. We even did a full sweep of the area, but turned up nothing."

"How many vehicles were there?" asked Greg.

"Ten, not counting their escorts. They even had a working Terrex with mounted MGs," replied Major Shang, referring to the Singapore-made amoured fighting vehicles which allowed for weapons platforms including grenade and rocket launchers. "Then, our original concern was that they were establishing a staging point to mount attacks on us. Our location was supposed to be secret, but we have had scavengers and soldiers go missing from time to time. But when nothing happened for months, we closed the case."

"The convoy didn't leave the area?" asked Greg.

"No sign of it. With what you said, I'm guessing they brought in computer equipment and a crew to work on the server you were talking about, maybe even power tools. You don't keep such a thing secure with plain wooden doors."

"But how do they resupply? They need food, water even."

"Tunnels. There's a shitload of them beneath the city," confirmed Captain Ping. "My patrol has been outside long enough to know that. Our best estimate is that over seventy percent of them are either collapsed or unexplored. Not to mention there are so many ways to hide an entrance. A slab of concrete, or even changing the locks to a door. Food and drink are easy to transport, but not high-level computer equipment. Chances are, all non-essential crew such as fighters are being rotated out this way. No one can stay in one place for too long without losing their mind."

"So what's the plan?" demanded Greg. "You'll excuse me for saying, but most of your men don't seem to care if this dump goes to hell."

The men at the table glared at him.

"Greg and his friend haven't exactly seen the best side of our community," said Ang carefully. "The guards on duty were, as you know, uncooperative as ever. It wasn't always like this."

"Morale has been bad for a while now," admitted Major Shang. "Few of the soldiers believe we would ever be attacked, not while we remain underground. But the types of food we can grow are limited, not just because of the lack of sunlight, but because there weren't many fruit trees around here in the first place. The soil we use for growing crops is also getting worse by the day. Bu the Colonel refuses to allow any foraging operations outside of the immediate area, and so we remain. You see all these faces around you? These are the ones who will fight with us."

"Does the Colonel allow it?" asked Greg.

"The Colonel will likely have the base on lockdown if any word of this gets out," said Major Shang. "But I am the OC of the Old Guard Commando Unit, and I have the authority to lead a battle group. Captain Ping and 3SG Ang are from the Scout Unit, but they have agreed to help us."

Greg nodded. Ang seemed like an okay guy. Captain Ping was, well, as careful as any responsible officer should be. "Do we have any intel on what to expect?" he asked. Already the experience he had in military exercises was kicking in. As a Military Expert in the SAF—a soldier with the vocation of engineer—ranked ME4, an officer rank equal to Captain, he sometimes had to take charge of company-level operations.

"Enemies are arriving by the truckload around the Gardens, and there appears to be mortar emplacements to the east," Major Shang turned the cardboard on the wall over, displaying a photocopy of the map of the area around them.

He picked up a stick of charcoal, marking a cross on an area on the right. "This is Gardens by the Bay. The facility you mentioned has got to be some ways underground, otherwise it would have been destroyed during The Storm. Mortar emplacements seem to be concentrated on the side of the river just across the Helix Bridge. For some reason, much of the bridge itself is still standing, so we should be able to make our way across it. Do any of you know where exactly the server is?"

"It gets power and cooling from the old dam system of

Marina Barrage, with supplementary power absorbed from sunlight by the Supertrees," confirmed Wesley. "We don't have an exact location, but according to the architectural plans, it can be accessed by means of an entrance either at Marina Barrage itself, or The Shoppes at Marina Bay. There are no other known entrances."

"Fuck." Major Shang flung the charcoal stick onto the table. The other soldiers looked on in silence.

"What's wrong?" asked Greg nervously.

"Marina Barrage is going to be crowded with 418, if our intel is anything to go by," grunted Major Shang. "Even if all our men were to be activated, we'll never be able to reach it without heavy losses. I'm sorry, but I don't think it's going to happen."

"Then we'll enter by The Shoppes," said Greg. He really didn't see what the problem was.

"It's home to an unknown number of Mindless."

Damn. Greg clenched his jaw, looking to Wesley. He didn't look confident at all. After that incident in the MRT tunnels, Greg wished never to encounter those things again. It wasn't just that they could rend you from limb to limb in an instant, there was something unsettling about their howls and snarls, sounds that came only from one's deepest nightmares. Tangling with one was the closest one could come to encountering monsters.

"What equipment do we have available?" asked Greg. Major Shang looked back in annoyance.

"Are you bloody kidding me? There's no way eight of my men are going through that! Do you know just how many of them there are? Hundreds! Maybe even well over a thousand!"

Several times a year, some IT show or other would be held at one of three locations throughout the nation: Singapore Expo, Suntec City's Convention and Exhibition Centre or Sands Expo and Convention Centre. These shows always attracted crowds of people. On opening days, when selected electronics could cost a fraction of their actual price, people would queue up overnight, so that queues snaked around the building.

Lots of people queuing out in the open, exposed to unhealthy bursts of cosmic radiation. Lots of Mindless created.

But Greg's son was there, deep in the bowels of the server facility, being subjected to who knows what. He couldn't turn back.

"Major, do you know the fate Guo Li narrowly escaped?" demanded Greg. Major Shang said nothing. "The 418 were about to install electronics into his head, and hook him up to a server system. Not to transfer data, but decrypt security protocols. Right now, this is happening to my son. Do you want to be an accessory to the 418's cruelty? Do you want to live on as the guy who sat by doing nothing, while defenceless kids had their brains fried? The choice is yours, Major."

Major Shang banged the table with two fists, and for a moment, Greg wondered if he had gone too far.

"Do you think we would knowingly let innocent kids die?" yelled the Major. "We of the Old Guard know what the 418 are capable of! We know of their Blood Arenas and slaves, of their penchant for violence and evil! But we are also the protectors of two thousand civilians, many of them women and children! You come here all high and mighty, full of righteousness and shit, telling us what we should or should not do! Well, the lives of a few cannot justify the lives of many. That's just the way it is."

"The 418 will not stop after getting the server's data," spoke Wesley. His tone, so different from Greg's, drew everyone's attention. "You think the shelling is bad? History has shown that power corrupts. They will use that knowledge to destroy your city, to flush you out like rats in a storm. They will enslave everyone who isn't killed, and put them to building new facilities and weapons they will learn about from the server. With those weapons, they will destroy whatever's left of your survivors. Hide like rats if you will, but the day will come when you can hide no longer."

That was by far the most eloquent speech Wesley had delivered. "If you won't come with us, that's understandable," said Greg. "We only ask that you return us our gear, and we'll be on our way. If it wasn't for our little tour through your city, that's how it should have been."

The room was quiet. Captain Ping broke the silence.

"When I first signed up, I did it to protect the innocent," said Captain Ping. "To defend the weak against the might of the strong. Then, it was threats to national security. But what is the point of loyalty to country if you don't even help a stranger in need? Greg and Wesley here saved our asses from the 418, with no idea if they were going to be taken to our base. In retrospect, a few of my men and I owe them our lives."

"As do I," said Sergeant Ang.

"With your leave, Major, I will show our guests where they may retrieve their gear." Captain Ping stood up. "Let's go, Ang."

"Not so fast," said Major Shang. Everyone, including the Captain and Sergeant, froze.

"Take two of our SAW retrofits with you," said the Major. "You'll need it to fight the Mindless. Those scum are as numerous as flies."

TO DANGER DEEP

Greg had originally worried that the ragtag excuse of an army didn't have much in the way of advanced weaponry. The usefulness of whatever weapons they had would be limited by modifications, such as electronic sights. But it seemed that there were some surprises in store for him.

The Ultimax 100 was one of the lightest SAWs on the planet, and in fact came close to being an assault rifle. The Singapore-made Squad Automatic Weapon proved that even a petite-sized person could fire an entire mag of ammunition single-handedly for sustained periods, owing to its highly manageable recoil. What the Old Guard Commandos had were new Gen 4 models, complete with Picatinny rails and a full optics package. Working electronics were a rarity, even more so were holographic sights and laser aiming devices that could actually be turned on. There was even a 40mm 3GL attached to the bottom rail. This was a grenade launcher capable of holding three 40mm rounds, which would be more than a little useful when handling tight groups. Much to the bafflement of the others, Wesley had opted for his AV-2 with GoPro mounting, so Ang got the other Ultimax. Together with the soldiers, Greg and Wesley donned

LBVs with both soft and hard ballistic armour plates, along with helmets made ten years ago. All these would fetch a fortune, if anyone ever offered it for sale in the wasteland. It would do little against the animalistic attacks of the Mindless, but would help immensely when facing the 418 defenders.

Major Shang checked everyone's gear one final time, and led them through a side corridor. He and his team had agreed to accompany them as far as half of the way to The Shoppes, and were similarly geared. They had to keep their heads down, as patrols roamed the halls regularly, but Greg doubted anyone remembered they existed. The tension in the air was palpable, thick as a fog. Lights had been dimmed, and Major Shang explained this was to reduce light leakages through the rubble from pinpointing their position. They went past a checkpoint with guards marginally more attentive than the previous ones, and were soon in the tunnels. Up they went through a locked maintenance hatch, and to Greg's surprise, he felt the breeze of fresh air. Well, as fresh as dusty city air could be. They were in the middle of a courtyard, enclosed by a half-circle collection of ruins. They were in the grounds of what was the Esplanade building and Greg could just make out what used to be bars and eateries. Scavengers had probably already been through them, if the owners hadn't already taken the contents with them. Alcohol cost a lot before The Storm, and would be worth far more after it happened.

"To the east of here is the old Floating Platform," whispered Major Shang. "We'll do a sweep around the immediate area, then get to the top of the seating area. From there, we can do a reconnaissance of what lies ahead." He patted the binoculars around his neck.

"Good plan. Will there be any 418 patrols about?" Greg

looked about. "It seems quiet, for now."

"The 418 weren't shelling the area randomly. We believe they have spotters who relayed the location of our patrols back to the mortar troopers." Major Shang looked around. "Now that most of our topside troops are now at base awaiting further orders, the shelling seems to have stopped. I don't think they'll be coming to clear us out anytime soon.

"That said, we have to tread carefully," the Major warned. "We don't have any thermal sighting devices left, but the 418 might. Dash when you are out in open spaces, and always keep behind cover. Understood?"

"Yes, Sir!" everyone breathed. "Follow my lead! Go go go!"

Major Shang dashed forward, and everyone followed after, split into two teams. Greg, Wesley, Ping and Ang had the call sign Hunter 1 to 4, while the others were Avenger 1 to 4. A mix of boots and sneakers rustled across the ground, sounding loud in the otherwise quiet night. They were on the move, and Greg couldn't help but feel the thrill of the hunt.

For too long, he had been in hiding, then oppressed by the 418, powerless to stop them. He had thought that escaping gave them less power over him, but in truth, he was simply escaping again, if only to find his son. The 418 had then seemed too powerful to fight against. But now he was out on the road, armed with the best equipment anyone could have, backed by several of the best fighters in the wasteland. It just felt great to be able to make a difference.

Hawkeye Zhen was always trying to make a difference. The life of 418 members had improved each time he found a cache of resources scavengers had overlooked. His superiors had attributed it to his keen sight and perceptiveness. He personally accorded it to his being thorough. Because of his inherent ability as a scout, the Red Pole of Operations had appointed him a Hawkeye. This meant more food for his family, and even a sizable space in the Brotherhood apartments.

During peacetime, Hawkeyes had one main job, to watch over an area of the city, bolt-action sniper rifle in hand. Any scavenger not bearing the 418 colours or tattoos was to be shot, with their location reported. The resources of the city were limited, and it wouldn't do any good to let pariahs have them.

When the Dragon Head himself declared war on the Old City, Hawkeyes now had a new role: calling in enemy troop movements to the boys handling the mortars. Where mortars couldn't reach, nearby patrols would deal with. A bolt-action sniper rifle was lethal against single targets, but against groups, it only served to draw danger towards oneself. Before The Storm, he had never ridden in the Singapore Flyer. He now got his wish, perched within one of the highest cabins, giving him a clear line of sight over much of the city. He recognised the sinking mass of the Floating Platform, where countless recruits who had completed Basic Military Training, including him, were force-marched to in a bid to remind them of their obligations. Well, he served a greater power now.

This was Zhen's third shift in a row. The Dragon Head had ordered that no rest was to be taken until the operation was complete. Loyalty was important, but it did little to ease the ache behind his eyes. Several times he dozed off, only to awaken in shock, aware that he could have been caught sleeping on duty. Unlike other 418 sub-units, Hawkeyes had no love for each other. Being a rare breed, they saw each other as competitors, and were more than willing to report laziness to their superior. Even up high as he was, all it would take was a good scope and a big mouth to get him in trouble.

Movement down below. Zhen blinked, wondering if it was a couple of overgrown trees shaking. This far into the city, no one dared to come merely to cut them down for wood.

Two teams of soldiers, almost invisible in the dimness of the night. They had gained quite a lot of ground in the time he had been musing. But nothing escapes a Hawkeye's sight for long. Shifting himself to a firing position, Zhen reached for his radio.

∎

Just as they were up against the wall of the Youth Olympics commemoration area, Major Shang held up a hand. Everyone stopped, dropping behind cover. A long whistle could be heard, getting steadily louder and louder.

"Get down!" yelled the Major, and everyone hit the ground. Hands were placed over necks, faces down with legs hastily crossed.

Greg had been military exercises utilising live rounds before, but nothing could have prepared him for this. An earthquake that shook his very chest and bones, resonating throughout his being. The volume of a hundred thunderstorms, all happening right beside him. He might have yelled, but couldn't hear it over the din. He could have been in purgatory, but couldn't see. Bits of concrete rained down upon his exposed hands, several making loud reports against his helmet and armour plates. A loud ringing persisted throughout his eardrums, and Greg was amazed they hadn't yet burst. His body felt sluggish, resisting his every move.

***

Hawkeye Zhen cursed as the dust erupted 15 metres away from the targets, levelling a couple of short concrete structures. The mortar's targeting systems must be faulty, to go so far off as that. But what wasn't after The Storm? Residual magnetism could last a long time.

"Volley wide! Volley wide!" he spoke quickly on the radio. "Compensate barrage by 15 metres left!"

"Walau eh!" came the reply, followed by a burst of static. It would take a while for those idiots to recalibrate their shots. Gripping his TRG-42 rifle, Zhen chambered a round, well-oiled bolt sliding effortlessly.

Electronics may fail without reason. But mechanical weapons rarely do.

***

Greg was vaguely aware of being dragged by his left arm, and staggered upright. The others were likewise dazed, but were stumbling onwards to the bridge that led across the river. He vaguely remembered there were supposed to be three bridges in total, one of them being a monstrosity of spiral steel.

"Get to the bridge!" yelled the commando grabbing onto him, and Greg nodded groggily.

The commando gurgled and fell. A loud report resounded across the city. The soldiers looked around in confusion, and fell quickly back to the ground. A couple of them swore in Hokkien.

"Sniper!" groaned Greg. He slid quickly behind a slab of concrete, right beside Wesley. The acolyte didn't seem disoriented by the mortar attack; rather, he looked more attentive than usual.

Another shot erupted, disintegrating a portion of concrete. Greg knew this wasn't the time to lose his nerve. But even against a large group, a sniper could prove dangerous. At the very least, they would be pinned down, and unable to move. At worst, some would try to flee in panic, making them vulnerable to fire.

"I'm picking up radio transmissions in the area," reported Wesley. "It's being transmitted between the sniper and the mortar teams. The signal's coming from the Ferris wheel!" The acolyte pointed at the Singapore Flyer. Several of the carriages were missing, but a few still stood.

"So which carriage is he in, then? What can we do?" Greg asked. "It's not like we can get a direct shot at him."

"Make good use of what you have. Necessity is the mother of improvisation."

■

Zhen yanked the bolt of his gun back, cursing. A puff of smoke curled out of the chamber before he rammed it back shut, aligning his crosshair on one of the running figures. He fired, throwing his target to the ground. As expected, the others looked stunned. If he kept this up, they would all scatter in due time. He only needed to hold them long enough for the mortar teams to get their act together.

One of the figures stood up, weapon held at the ready. Fool. He couldn't possibly see where the firer was, and yet he exposed himself for a shot. Zhen set his sights on that guy's head.

The firer's gun jerked, surprising Zhen mentally, his finger pausing at the trigger. A loud explosion sounded, the carriage he was in erupting in flames, metal and glass disintegrating. The carriage pitched forward and fell.

Zhen screamed as he saw the ground rushing towards him, the sound of creaking and tearing metal loud in his ears.

Despite being hundreds of metres away, everyone felt the vibration of the carriage crashing onto the ground, the sound echoing far into the night. No more sniper fire could be heard, at least for now.

"Everyone okay?" yelled Major Shang. "Sound off!"

"Hunter 1 to 4, clear!" yelled Captain Ping, looking quickly at his men.

"Avenger 2 and 4 are down!" yelled the commando known as Zari. "Avenger 1 and 3 remaining!"

"Fuck," began the Major. "We have to advance across the bridge now! There'll soon be 418 heading towards us."

"You said you'll escort us as far as the bridge," reminded Greg. He dusted off his hands. He was glad for the Nomex gloves he was provided. Any cuts he sustained could be easily infected.

"I didn't expect this clusterfuck to happen. By the look of things, you're going to need our help anyway." Major Shang turned to Zari. "You still with us?"

"Yes, Sir!"

"Go! Cover to cover on the bridge!"

There used to be three bridges, two for vehicles, but they had long since collapsed due to the effects of The Storm. This left only the Helix Bridge. Crafted out of stainless steel, the Helix Bridge was supposed to depict the human DNA structure, with various symbols representing the four DNA bases affixed at different points of the bridge. Greg had personally thought it looked like an overgrown series of creepers, more akin to representing Singapore's ever-increasing population. In many of the places he had travelled to, any sizeable metal structure such as statues and railings had been sawn off or otherwise removed to be melted down for the precious materials they provided. To have such a large quantity of untouched stainless steel was an extremely rare sight, and could qualify as one of the wonders of the post-Storm world. Leaping over the plastic barricades that had been set up years ago for some event or other, the soldiers dashed onwards, boots and shoes clopping on the concrete.

A circular blob of white light flew high in the sky, bathing everything in a bright radiance.

"Illumination flare! Get down!" yelled Captain Ping, but he needn't have bothered. Everyone's training had kicked in, sending them hugged close to the floor of the bridge.

Machine gun fire erupted through the night, sporadic tracers indicating their line of fire. The 7.62mm bullets ricocheted off the metallic sides of the bridge, creating a cacophony of squeals and clanks. It was terrifying, to say the least, and Greg was all too aware of how little cover the bridge presented. There were viewing decks at the sides where they could duck into, but they were spaced about 20 metres from each other. Two ice cream carts could be seen, as well as what appeared to be a dustbin. One could only hope they weren't as flimsy as the usual stuff made in China.

"To the sides! To the sides!" yelled Major Shang, and the rest didn't need telling twice. One of the viewing decks was near enough that they could duck inside it, but every good soldier knew getting clustered together is bad news. A single explosive could take them all out.

"Anyone got any smoke?" asked Greg. A burst shattered several light fittings overhead, and he was glad for his goggles and helmet.

"I do, but it won't work here. Bridge's too narrow," said Ang. "They can just shoot within the narrow space and get us anyway. Maybe we can use a 40mm?"

"Nabei, they've got to be at least 500 metres away! Well out of range!" Captain Ping looked around. "Anyone got a sniper rifle?"

"It fell with Santosh back there," confirmed Major Shang. "The sniper got him first."

"So we lost our sniper support. What do we do?" demanded Captain Ping. He risked a peek over his cover. "We better be prepared, 'cause a couple of tattoos are coming up fast."

"Their mortars use electronic targeting," said a voice dreamily. Greg turned. Of all the times, Wesley was swaying side by side, his hand touching the steel of the bridge. His AV-2 carbine hung loosely from its strap beside him.

"What?" demanded Greg. "Wesley, we don't have time for this. The 418 are coming. Get your shit together and prepare yourself."

"I can tap into their communications. There are electronic targeting systems and ammunition close by," slurred Wesley. "The Cloud will set things right."

The Helix Bridge was a large metal structure, and it was then that Greg knew it could also function as a giant antenna, especially with an acolyte of the BOC in contact with it. He turned to yell at the rest to brace themselves.

A series of booms went off one after another, shaking the very submerged foundations of the bridge. Just six years prior, the last series of fireworks had gone off in the same area for

National Day, an event which took the better part of a few months to prepare. Only now, the explosions were far quicker in succession, with the city lit up in flashes of orange and red, rather than the more varied colours every Singaporean was used to. The other side of the river billowed with an almost otherworldly light, and some would say it was the fires of Hell itself. And in its way, it was. The screams of the MG and mortar operators couldn't be heard at this distance, but even up close, the roar of explosives would have drowned them out. Interspersed in the midst of the red and orange inferno were flashes of white and green, mostly likely the illumination and signalling mortar shells going up in flames too. Wesley had had less than a minute to prepare, and yet the lightshow before them was more professional than could be expected. In the far distance, another series of explosions could be seen, lighting up part of the skyline. The mortar tubes in another area were going up in flames as well.

And then it was over. All that was left was a series of bonfires lining the side of the Singapore River. If one didn't know that a mass detonation had taken place, it could have just been business as usual by the riverside, the year before The Storm laid claim to all there was. And what was more business as usual now with men of different interests trying to kill one another?

Some things never changed.

The other side of the Helix Bridge was a huge mess. Although it was estimated from the debris that no more than four mortar guns were assembled, it seemed that a large stockpile of ammunition had caused a chain reaction. One person was still wandering in a daze, shreds of what looked to be an ILBV fused to his bloodied frame. His skin was so badly fried that no one could identify his tattoos or ethnicity.

"Put him down," ordered Major Shang. Zari nodded, jerking his SAR 21 towards him. A bang resounded through the night.

"What a mess," whistled Captain Ping. Chunks of the solid granite tiles that had lined the riverside were thrown up during the tumult. The side of The Shoppes facing the bridge had collapsed, glowing ends of rebar and metal framework indicating what had transpired. "To think that I wanted to shop here once."

"But we survived! We fucking survived!" laughed Ang.

"Keep your fucking voices down!" snapped Major Shang. "418 could have sent troops to search the area. Besides, we don't know how many Mindless are in there. And will someone please tell me what the hell just happened?"

This was directed towards Greg and Wesley. "It's rather hard to explain," said the acolyte.

"You just caused military-grade munitions to detonate, NDP-style. Manufacturers test that crap to ensure shit like this doesn't happen by accident. What. The. Fuck. Happened." Major Shang crossed an arm over his rifle, glaring through his goggles.

Greg cleared his throat. "Major, the important thing is that we—"

"We?" the Major exclaimed. "That's the point, isn't it? 'We' includes the people who are accompanying you on your little jaunt. 'We' comprises the ones who had braved fire from mortar teams, only to have said teams consumed by what can only be described as Heavenly Fire. Life may be common, but my men's lives are precious, so you'll understand if I wish to know the capabilities of the ones we're dealing with."

There was an uncomfortable silence, during which the four remaining soldiers stared down Greg and Wesley.

"I used high-frequency propagation to tap onto the local 418 radio frequency, and detonate the electrically-primed munitions," said Wesley finally. "That's all there is to it."

"What?" exclaimed Ang and Captain Ping in confusion.

"It's rather hard to explain to those who aren't versed in electronics and computer science—"

"Enough," said Major Shang as Captain Ping flashed Wesley the finger. "Can you do it again?"

"I've used much of my internal power reserves to do that, not to mention detonating another cache at Marina Barrage," said Wesley. "But when my power's recharged through my kinetic motors and power bank, I might just be able to pull it off again. I'll need a large-sized antenna to do that."

"We have a superweapon with us then," said Major Shang. The veteran was either incapable of smiling, or unwilling to. Why, Greg couldn't figure. "That means we can fight anything the 418 throws at us, be it artillery, mortar or cannon fire. Do you agree, men?" He looked around at the soldiers.

"To the ends of the Nation, Sir!" they chorused.

"Then we check our weapons and move," Major Shang said, reloading his SAR 21 MMS. "We have Mindless to watch out for."

▪

Like Ion Orchard, The Shoppes at Marina Bay wasn't so much a mall as a place for shoppers to view designer brands they would otherwise never be able to see, hold or touch. Despite Greg walking through the mall with his wife countless times before, they had never bought anything in there, not unless he counted tickets to *Les Misérables* and *The Lion King*. Even the prices at the food court were exorbitant.

Perhaps that was how the management broke even with the rent. Not that it mattered now, when property and COE values were down to pretty much zero. Things that were most valued now? Working guns and weapons. Competent guys to gather and use them. Clean water. Palatable food.

For now, Greg could say he was pretty much a millionaire in wasteland terms, with four gun-toting Old Guard soldiers and a computer cultist to back him up. They even had a half-full SAF water bottle each, with dried bread as night snacks and emergency rations. He wielded a 4th-Generation Ultimax 100 SAW that would probably jam somewhere along the line, but had proven capable of firing rounds quickly with accuracy.

The only thing he was missing was his son, and that would soon be set right.

Dark gaping storefronts stared silently out at them, with signage inside indicating their previous occupants—the likes of Hermès, Chanel and Gucci. It was these stores that had been broken into, while stores such as 7-Eleven and those selling food and local brands were untouched. The looters sure knew their priorities.

"It's too damn quiet here," commented Ang. "I thought Mindless would be crawling all over us as soon as they hear the explosions."

"They hate the light and loud noises. They're probably holing up somewhere in the basements," answered Zari. Their footsteps were punctuated by the soft crunch of glass underfoot.

"Quiet! We have to get downstairs," hissed Major Shang.

"The door to the server lies below." Switching to a two-astride formation, the six of them stepped their way carefully down the escalators, boots click-clacking down the rusted steel steps.

Being a considerably short building, The Shoppes suffered relatively little destruction, with only the shattered glass of its outer facade betraying what happened. If society ever got back to normalcy, one could probably refit the large amount of floor area into fields of crops, and the shops into living spaces. It was prime real estate for the 418, and yet it remained untouched by the major powers in the wasteland, a place trapped forever in the past.

There were starting to be signs of another presence as they got to the artificial canal in Basement Two. A rancid odour permeated the air the deeper they got, with distant sounds of what sounded like scrabbling. Everyone was all nerves, flicking their weapons left and right, but for all the gloom, none of them could make out anything.

"It's as dark as a tunnel down here," whispered Captain Ping. "Sir, I suggest we turn on our torches, or pretty soon we're going to walk into a hole in the ground."

"Very well. Lights on."

Everyone reached for the torches taped to their weapons. A mix of incandescent and LED beams lit up the area.

The first thing they noticed were the misshapen spots littered throughout the ground, brown and yellow lumps that could best be described as many digested meals. This presumably gave off the stench they were breathing in. Yellow pools were similarly interspersed throughout the area, and Greg noted with disgust that he had stepped onto one. If he didn't know any better, he would have thought he was in a zoo enclosure or slum.

But a light breathing could be heard in the artificial canal that cut through the middle of the basement. Training his weapon beam upon it, Greg saw something that proved all this wasn't the work of mere animals.

The canal used to be about a metre deep with water, and one could take boat rides on it for a fee. Now it was waist deep with stack upon stack of bones and crouching Mindless, all tensed like men waiting in a trench.

Like men waiting for the signal to attack.

Greg backed away, but an exclamation from behind him broke the silence.

"Mindless! Kill! Kill them all!" screamed Ang. He let loose a volley from his SAW.

In such an enclosed space, the noise was deafening, echoing throughout the endless halls of the complex. But if gunfire was deafening, the combined screech of all the Mindless was the most terrifying thing any of them had ever heard.

Storefronts shattered as Mindless burst out of hiding, dressed in a mix of rags and adornments. Several more dropped from the floors above, where they'd been minding their own business. Those in the canal nearest to Ang were shredded by his gunfire, while the rest poured out by the sides.

"Fire at will!" roared Major Shang, and four other weapons added to the chorus. One of the Mindless got hold of Zari, but the commando rifle-butted its head in. Greg shot down the two closest to him, pausing briefing to activate one of the homemade grenades he had gotten. He flicked the disposable lighter attached to the jar, lobbing it towards the far end of the hall. The basement lit up briefly as a smoky flame erupted, setting several charging attackers on fire. Not quite as good as frag grenades, but good enough to set scum on fire.

"Move, move, move!" ordered the Major as he dashed

forward, MMS at the ready. Everyone spaced themselves out from each other, boots thudding as they leapt over the corpses of slain Mindless. They fired burst after sporadic burst as Mindless broke out of side passageways and public toilets; there was no telling how many more remained. Some of the Mindless that had been shot limped and crawled after them, their feral instincts overriding their pain. They posed far less of a threat, but a stray bite could still prove fatal in days if left untreated and allowed to fester.

"The door that leads to the facility is just up ahead! Just a little while more!" encouraged Major Shang. "Keep it up, boys!"

"How far away?" asked Greg. He swapped his drum magazine for another, the heat of his gun noticeable even through his gloves. Wesley, on the other hand, seemed unfazed, like this was just a guided tour to him. But if what he said was to be believed, he had already seen more horrors than Greg had in the mines. Fighting Mindless had to come second nature to him.

"You remember where the underground casino is? That's where," said Major Shang he fired at the heads of one, then two Mindless.

"A casino? Are you fucking kidding? Why there of all places?" spluttered Greg.

"A server farm of this magnitude needs a high security access point." Major Shang hunkered down against a marble pillar and peered out into the passageway. "What better security than a casino or bank vault? MBS probably brokered a deal to get some computational power for their machines."

"That must explain why the probability of striking it big is null," commented Wesley.

"You would know, wouldn't you?" teased Greg.

"I am a servant of the Code. Probabilities and numbers are my life."

"No I meant—" Greg shook his head. "Never mind."

"If you are implying that I was a gambler here, then yes, I do confess I was here once—"

"Can you both shut up here?" snapped Captain Ping with a scowl. The blood and gore coating his goggles and helmet did nothing to soften it. "We're fighting for our lives and yet we still have to hear this bullshit."

Greg looked at Wesley, but the acolyte didn't roll his eyes or do anything like that. But if he could emote digitally, he would probably say "~.~" or ">.<".

There didn't seem to be any more Mindless for the time being, but Greg wouldn't put it past even brain-fried beings to fall back and regroup. They had to have adopted some kind of pack mentality, like the spotted hyena; otherwise they would have killed each other a long time ago. The old signs were still around, and Greg saw with relief that they had now reached the casino in the basement.

There was a series of turnstiles at the casino's entrance, and long ago, all Singapore citizens had to pay an entrance fee of a hundred dollars. Greg had never gone inside, since he didn't consider bankruptcy and despair as desirable states. Now that money was virtually worthless, and there weren't any guards to demand a token fee of food or ammo, the six of them hopped the turnstiles for free. The crinkle of unwanted and unused chips on the floor was satisfying, a snub at careless spending while people of these days lived with barely enough food to get by. Glasses and goblets still sat where they were abandoned, their contents long since dried or downed. With the prices of alcohol as they were, it was more likely the latter than former.

A thick layer of dust had gathered around everything, with the beams of the lights emphasising the dust motes in the air. Hues of green, blue and amber were lit up as the light settled across the bar, many of its bottles toppled or missing, Slot machines sat unused and unwanted since the prospect of striking it big lost its importance. Either that, or the chips within were all gone. Several suited and smartly-dressed skeletons lounged or otherwise lay in sofas or chairs, some with glasses or cigarettes in hand.

"Do you all hear something?" asked Zari nervously. A dull thumping, almost like there was something trapped in the walls. Greg saw the soldiers glancing at the skeletons littering the place, and understanding dawned upon him. Army guys were superstitious, if not more so than the average person.

"Come on, let's be realistic, guys," said Greg. "There's probably another reason for all that, like the metal of the shafts contracting and expanding. Where are we going, Major Shang?"

The officer snapped out of his thoughts. "It's just this way," he said. They came to an area where game tables were set, unfinished card games laying upon them. Many of the chip piles were absent, but gathered into heaps next to the exchange counters, as if the players had tried to exchange them but found the counter staff missing. A steel gate behind the counter had already been broken into, and for a moment, Greg held his breath, wondering if the 418 had already come before. But no, the dust on the floor was undisturbed, and when they entered, the imposing circle of the vault door was still intact, several scratches at the side showing looters had made a pathetic attempt to get into it. The vault door had to be 30cm thick, at least, and its locking bolts were made to stand up to almost anything.

"Break out the C4, Ang," ordered Captain Ping. Ang opened his utility pouch, handling out several bricks of plastic explosive.

"Begging your pardon, Captain, but I don't think that's going to work too well," said Greg. "We'll need thermite to melt through the bolts that thick—"

"Which is something we don't have," cut in Major Shang. "Resources are scarce, and it's not like the factory producing it is still in business. Get the blasting caps inside the C4 and we'll soon be in."

A grate fell off the ceiling, landing hard onto the bare floor with a clank. All of them turned towards it.

First one, then more of the Mindless tumbled out of it, screeching and spitting. The soldiers fired at them without flinching, too well-conditioned to hesitate, round casings clinking upon the concrete floor. Then two more grates at the side burst open, and they finally discovered the cause of the thumping.

The Mindless had been tracking them through the vents.

A group of four leapt upon Ang, and he fell down screaming. Greg swung the barrel of his weapon towards them, but his SAW chose to jam there and then, a dull clack resounding through hot steel. Having no other weapon except a knife, he tugged hard at the bolt of his weapon, splitting the offending round casing with a clink. He pulled the trigger as he charged forward, shredding the Mindless before him.

When he got to Ang, he saw that he was too late. The soldier's face was all but gone, his jaw hanging off what was left of his lower skull. The skin on his arms were so badly clawed and ripped that none of the sleeves of his uniform remained. Only his helmet and armour prevented his upper skull and torso from being assaulted, but now it was just adornment, for all the good it did.

"Get the rest of the C4 and move!" yelled Major Shang, throwing Greg back to the present.

Greg would have preferred a chance to say goodbye, but there wasn't time. More Mindless were pouring out as the men stopped briefly to reload, so he grabbed all of the rectangular charges with one hand. By the time he dashed to the door, Major Shang had already set a series of charges, not on the door itself, but where the locking bolts would be. A round vault door didn't have just a single bolt like a normal door, but could have as many as 24 of them. And the steel-lined concrete that made up its doorframe was extremely tough, and they would need all the explosives they could get. Greg tossed the rest to Major Shang before going over to help the other three.

Captain Ping was wounded in the arms, but was otherwise fine. Zari was uninjured so far, probably on account of his better commando training. He was striking out with a kitchen knife taped as a crude bayonet upon his SAR 21 barrel, so it must have jammed or ran out of ammo. Wesley fired in single shots, each one precise and deadly upon the Mindless' skulls. The polymeric barrel of his gun seemed to be giving off a lot of smoke, however. Despite the pile of Mindless bodies stacking up, with several blocking the vents to the left and right, the flow through the main door was relentless. Greg whipped out his second-last firebomb, flinging it against them. It failed to ignite, and he realised that in his haste, he hadn't flicked the switch.

"Prepare for breach!" yelled Major Shang. The four defenders dashed to the sides of the room and ducked, hands over ears.

A bang resounded throughout the air, and even with his ears closed, the ringing in his head hurt like hell. A thunderous shaking of the ground followed shortly, and Greg was aware of himself falling hard to the side, against the debris-lined floor.

He felt a hand pull at his shoulder, and looked groggily at him. Wesley was mouthing something at him, but for some reason, he couldn't hear. Then Wesley lifted up his sleeve and gripped his bare arm, and the familiar sensation of his electronic healing took effect. As his hearing returned, so did the damn ringing inside his head.

"Get up, Greg! You aren't passing out on us just yet!" said the acolyte. Greg looked behind him, and saw what had caused it all. The vault door had been blown off its bolts and hinges, landing face down on the ground. Weighing tens of tons at the very least, the impact of it had caused the ground to shake, throwing everyone down. Several of the Mindless were flattened by the door, with the others nowhere to be seen. Perhaps they're not as dumb as they made out to be, having fled from a noise that could shake the heavens. Already Major Shang and the rest were getting up with looks of pain upon their faces, blood-streaked but none too worse for wear, considering they'd almost been eaten by Mindless.

"My head," groaned Greg.

"Yep. Make that the whole lot of us." Again, Wesley didn't seem too fazed by what happened. Greg wondered just how many types of combat simulations he had experienced during his time with the BOC. Or for that matter, what horrors had he seen in the wasteland. He would have to ask him about it sometime.

They stepped into the vault. It was separated into two halves by fencing, with the centre area being a path where a trolley could be pushed. It was surprisingly bare aside from the bags of coins at the side. It seemed that in the wake of The Storm, people still believed that money still held value, and grabbed whatever they could carry.

At the end of the pathway was a steel door similar to that at the entrance of a HDB building's bomb shelter. Not as impressive as the door they had just blown off its hinges, but a solid metal door nonetheless. Fortunately, this one was secured by something far less fancy: two enormous Abloy padlocks, and a built-in deadbolt.

"Our guns and bolt cutters wouldn't work on these, but stick our remaining C4 on them, and we should be inside pretty soon," Major Shang was saying to Captain Ping. "Ah, glad you could join us, Greg."

This was it. Beyond this door lay the passageway to the server farm, no doubt full of 418 elite soldiers. Far better equipped, and all prepared to fight to the death.

The soldiers around him looked exhausted, with streaks of gore all over them. They had all gone on this mission without knowing if they would even make it across the river, much less succeed. All of the soldiers had risked their lives for Greg's son and whoever else was held in the server facility, for kids they didn't know. A few of them, including two commandos and Ang, had given up their lives in the process, two of them killed by an enemy they could never anticipate. Maybe that was what being the SAF or the Old Guard was all about. About fighting not just for those you know, but for those you don't.

"Thank you all for doing this," said Greg, and the soldiers looked at him. Even Wesley showed signs of surprise. "All of you here have people counting on you back home, and yet you came along with me. My original plan was to make it to the server with just Wesley—who is a true lifesaver—I must add, and handle what may come. I cannot ask any of you to risk your lives any further. If you would like to return to base, I have no argument with that."

The soldiers merely stared back at him.

"You really that siao or what?" Captain Ping finally said.

"What?" Greg sure didn't expect an answer like that.

"We've survived sniper and GPMG fire, shelling by mortars, fighting horde after horde of siaokia zombies, and now you tell us to turn back?" asked Captain Ping. "Sure, I have a wife and two kids, but in my line of work, I expect my life to be at risk. We're fighting for a greater purpose here, Greg. Something bigger than ourselves and our families."

"Remember when I said my men and I will lead you as far as the bridge?" reminded Major Shang. Greg nodded quietly. "That was the original plan. But my men and I had an agreement. Should the situation be far bigger than anything the four of you can handle, my men and I will fight alongside you. If Captain Ping and Sergeant Ang of the Scout Unit didn't hesitate to help, how could we?"

"What about Guo Li?" asked Greg.

"Guo Li needs a guardian, but even more than that, he and the other children need a world they can grow up safely in," said Major Shang. "The 418 is a scourge that we may never have the power to put down, but we can disrupt the ways and means in which they seek control. This includes their control of the server. If I have to die for there to be a better world, so be it." He hefted the Ultimax 100 he had retrieved from Ang.

Greg had braved through the last two weeks, not to help anyone else, but in the hope to save all that was left of his family. He had signed on as an SAF soldier back in the day, not just for the money, but for doing what he believed in. All those principles were lost when The Storm happened, and humanity was no longer about helping each other, but how one best helped oneself.

Six years it had been. Six years people played a game of the survival of the fittest. Perhaps it was not too late for him to do this not only for his son, but for all the people who had ever been enslaved or abused by the 418.

And these soldiers didn't question it. Even with their lives and their family on the line. Who was he to be any different?

"Let's do this!" Greg breathed, and together, he and the others checked and reloaded their weapons, clicks and clacks splitting the air. They had a fight ahead of them. A fight that would determine not just the fate of these particular children, but of those who would inherit the world.

BATTLE FOR SINGAPORE
(AND PERHAPS THE WORLD)

Abloy padlocks were notoriously hard to cut and pick, but not altogether hard to blow apart. Whenever they put their mind to it, mankind was capable of destroying anything.

Which led Greg to believe that should he put his mind to it, he would be able to kill every last motherfucker who believed in the glories of the 418. It was hard not to, charging through the door with fully-automatic weapon in tow, followed shortly by similarly-armed comrades.

The 418 weren't expecting anyone to come in through the back door, and so a couple of 49ers had wondered what the loud bangs were. The server farm was full of electronics, and so many things could go off after being powered up years later.

The bullets hit them hard and fast, and they were dead before they hit the floor. Even the maze of passageways of an underground facility filled with a constant hum of countless electronic and mechanical machines did little to muffle the harsh clatter of automatic firearms.

Greg kept his Ultimax raised as he looked around, taking in the surroundings. Row upon row of housing units stood about head-high, random flashes of LED lights lighting up their complicated surfaces. The flash of interface screens, lines upon lines of commands and text glowed dimly behind dusty screens. A whirring of fans could be heard, no doubt to cool the immense heat generated by the data processors. Indeed, the air carried a coolness Greg vaguely recognised as air-conditioning, a luxury that was lost six years prior. So many electronics in any one place, untouched and unsullied by The Storm. Even the 418 Labs were nothing compared to this. It was enough to make Greg's mind spin. But a look at Wesley confirmed this was nothing to him. He had probably seen this exact scene before in a SAF server somewhere.

"What exactly are we looking for?" asked Major Shang.

"This is just one of the many subprocessor units. The 418 wouldn't be able to access the server's decryption protocols from them," confirmed Wesley. "We need to get to the Control Room. It's the only way external interfaces can be connected to the system's network."

"Can help us Google translate or not?" asked Zari.

Wesley shot him a look. "It means that if you want to configure any server parameters, or connect stuff like thumb drives or laptop computers, you can only do it in that room."

"Do we have to worry about any of the stuff around us?" asked Captain Ping, scanning the area like the rest were. "I wouldn't like to get a bullet into anything that'll cause a total server shutdown or explosion."

"A server farm of this size has regular scheduled backups and redundancies. Just don't shoot anything if you don't need to." Greg was sure Wesley was rolling his eyes behind his goggles.

They came up to a large entranceway which had stairs leading up over an incline. From where they stood, nothing could be seen in the room beyond. In it, server cabinets housing standard 19-inch racks could be seen, along with what looked like hastily set up barricades of plastic and metal desks. A catwalk hung above the room, pipes of several colours running past it. Greg was reminded of a photo he'd seen of a Google Data Centre before, with pipes in green, yellow and red, the colours of their parent company. All these fed water to cool their servers. No one could be seen, and the only sign anyone had been around was the open olive-green-and-black military-grade cases at the side.

Cases that bore the Explosives Hazard symbol.

"Get to cover!" yelled Greg, already swinging behind the edge of the entrance. A loud explosion rang out, followed by the whistling of hundreds upon hundreds of metal shards directed in a conical arc. Being right at the front, Zari and Captain Ping were caught by the blast of several Claymores, falling backwards in sprays of blood. Ignoring the sting of the fragments as they bounced off the sides of walls and showered him, Greg stuck his head out quickly, eyeing the catwalk. Already the 418 soldier was discarding his detonator, whipping out a familiar egg-shaped object as he remained behind a crate for cover. One of the newer SAF-standard issue grenades, the five-metre blast radius would easily eliminate them before they had a chance to break cover. Without taking the time to think, Greg levelled his SAW's underbarrel launcher at him and fired, the characteristic "phunk" resounding through the air.

The blast that came immediately rivalled the Claymores. A segment of the catwalk came crashing down, the 418 soldier following it with a scream. Greg advanced quickly into the room with Wesley.

"Sector clear," Wesley reported calmly, AV-2 held by his hip.

"Room clear!" Greg confirmed. They were in a crossroads of the entire compound, with passageways leading to the front, left, and right. Greg was rather surprised there weren't more men guarding this area, but those might have been the ones he and the Old Guard shot down earlier. Caught in a bind, the last 49er must have tried holding the line by himself. "What's the status of the wounded, Major?"

"Zari's dead," said Major Shang, his voice breaking. "Ping's alive, but I'm not sure if he's going to make it."

Greg dashed back to where the two motionless figures lay. There wasn't much of Zari's face left, and judging by the amount of blood, he had taken the brunt of the blasts. A standard Claymore mine had a lethal range of over 50 metres, but the blasts had been less than 10 metres away. Major Shang hadn't got away unscathed, with one of his cheeks marked with red. Captain Ping lay on his back, wheezing hard as he clutched his chest. Crimson rivulets rolled down his forehead. Major Shang had pulled out a roll of makeshift bandages, but the Captain was refusing to let him remove his ILBV.

"Ping, your wound—"

"Save it. You guys are going to need it later," gasped the Captain. "There's no hope left for me. Go. Go before it's too late."

"We're not going to leave you," said Greg. "Wesley, can you do anything for Ping?"

Wesley shook his head. "Not through Calibration, no. It doesn't heal open wounds quickly enough. Besides, the shrapnel's still inside and we don't have a safe and clean place to remove that." Infection set in easily in the wasteland, except in the cleanest environments.

"I'm not going to let you suffer, Ping," said Major Shang, pulling out a pistol.

A soft laughter resounded in the chamber. For a moment, Greg thought it was coming from the Captain, his mind breaking under stress. When the next sentence came, however, he realised it was coming from the far corner of the room. The 418 soldier he had brought down had spoken where he lay, head tilted towards them.

"Pain is but a sign of the end, the suffering that precedes quest's end." Despite looking little more than a corpse himself, the 49er still carried some life yet within him. "Oh, you think you have suffered, but no, suffering is what the others were undergoing before you came." He broke down in a fit of the giggles, blood pooling around his lips in a ghastly grin.

Greg walked up to him. "You have a nerve opening your fat mouth after blasting us."

"Merely warning you of what lies ahead. The kids must be in so much pain, twitching, screaming … "

Greg slammed the heel of his boot upon the 49er's abdomen, eliciting a gasp, and then the butt of his weapon against his open fingers. As the thug made to crawl away, Greg held him still with a boot, barrel of the gun shoved against his temple.

"What are you fucks doing to them?" yelled Greg. "Where are they now?"

"The programmers … are decrypting … the Allspace … Machine," gasped the 49er, his speech impeded by the pressure exerted upon him. "Kids connected to it … so much twitching … "

"Where?" The boot pressed harder. The gasp turned into a croak, and Greg eased his pressure just a little.

"Straight … ahead …" The 49er pointed with a finger, then turned still. His sightless eyes remained open, never to close again.

Greg walked back to where Major Shang stood with Wesley. What he saw there was worth more than any words. Captain Ping looked tiredly back at them, as relaxed as anyone could be.

"I've just given him a neurorelaxant," said Wesley, showing Greg a small plastic packet, a needle affixed atop it. "It's normally reserved for disciples of the Code to better connect to the divinities, but I have discretion. He won't be in any pain for the next three hours. It was that, or a bullet through the head."

"Major Shang, perhaps you can bring Captain Ping—" began Greg.

"We'll get him out when all this is fought and done," affirmed Major Shang. "At this point, you'll going to need all the help you can get."

"What about Guo Li?" asked Greg. "He needs you."

"What about Jin? He needs us to save him."

Greg afforded himself a pained smile. "When all this is done, Colonel Beng had better give you a medal."

"I'd rather have a month's worth of three meals, thank you very much. Colonel Beng always was a stingy fuck." Major Shang gave his weapon one last check. "Shall we?"

The 418 was at the forefront of technology, in wasteland terms. They continuously researched sustenance living, military technology and renewable energies. Those who didn't know any better would say the 418 were just a community of thugs who saw their chance to take over the moment society broke down.

Research Master La-Zu was one of the longest-serving members of the 418. One of the few professors considered skilled enough by the 418 for developmental research, he had been working in Fusionopolis long before The Storm. Each time he made a new discovery, the computer infrastructure company he worked for took the developmental rights and credit instead of him. Naturally, when the one he would eventually know as Dragon Ho took over, and asked who was willing to serve him, La-Zu was the first to jump at the chance. He served the 418 well too, modifying salvaged electronics into working communications devices. He set up the interconnected radio network that formed the bulk of communications in the 418, with his designs used as far away as the mines in Johor. Granted, there were 418 territories further north, but he had yet to find out where. The 418 may seem ruthless in their task, but to La-Zu, their goals were just. They sought to rebuild a society from the ashes of what once was, recovering technology and salvageable computers. With much of the knowledge of how things were designed and made since been lost, a cache of digital data was most welcome. With the 418 being the closest thing to a government, La-Zu figured their existence was justified. They needed to expand, and if people had to be brought to their knees for that to happen, so be it. Finding the last remaining technology took priority over a false sense of freedom.

Then, about a year ago, the 418 made a discovery. The name of a location kept showing up on a number of classified documents originating from different governmental organisations. Based on the associated resources and computer terminology referring to it, it was believed a complete data centre existed beneath the Marina Bay area. With Singapore being a regional hub for many fields of technology, it would have made perfect sense.

An expedition was undertaken with the support of 1 Motors, a motor company of the 418.

La-Zu accompanied them as a senior researcher, along with his team. A couple of them were part of his original team before The Storm, with the rest new hires by the 418. The purported defenders of Marina Bay didn't give them any resistance, so it was as easy as the company splitting up into teams, and searching the depths of the tunnels beneath the city. And did they hit the motherlode.

The Allspace Server, or AS for short, dwarfed the capabilities of any other data centre in the world. Rather than simply relying upon rows upon rows of server cabinets to make up its processing power, the bulk of the AS's capability came from the hundreds of supercomputers and mainframes networked together, each running on multiple threads and quantum processors to maximise their capabilities. Supercomputers and mainframes had a high reliability rate, and afforded no more than a few minutes of downtime each year. And with so many networked together, it was a machine that could delegate its processes efficiently and quickly. Large amounts of stored data could be transferred quickly by any means, even wirelessly within the space of several minutes.

This would have been a turning point in the 418's technological capabilities, but yet there lay one problem. Having been designed as a store of not just commercial, but military and law enforcement data, the encryption built into its firmware was practically unbreakable. It took months to estimate the hardware and software requirements to even begin the process of decrypting what lay within. La-Zu even had several salvaged supercomputers from MINDEF and the National University of Singapore work on decryption subroutines, but it would still take years for it to happen.

The Dragon Head didn't want to wait a year. He wanted

results in a matter of months. For all the manpower they had, the 418 leader was pissed La-Zu and the other PhDs didn't have what it took. If they were really so smart, what was so difficult about decrypting code created by another person just like them? Perhaps the 418 should have La-Zu and his guys replaced with 10-year-olds instead?

The Dragon Head didn't know it then, but he had given La-Zu an idea. He had heard about how the brains of children are more adaptive, and how much quicker it learns when set upon a task. The 418 didn't have a shortage of people they could make use of, so he relayed his request to the Red Pole of the Laboratories.

The response was better than expected. Every week, a total of five children were sent to him. They were chosen for their abilities in mathematics or problem-solving, and only a limited number were taken from each territory to reduce the chance for revolt and population decline. A relatively happy community was a productive one. It was only a matter of installing the necessary analogue-to-digital implants for the subjects to be able to connect with the server's input interface. When connected, the subjects' implants would automatically run a decryption protocol, using their minds as a processor speed multiplier. He referred to them as Decryption Catalysts, or DCs.

For about a month now, he had put the minds of the DCs against the access mainframe, starting off with just one, then three. When the subjects started shaking and screaming, with their brains scrambled beyond the point of recovery, it was apparent that not enough decrypting power was used. More interfaces were set up, and more subjects brought in. There was even a kid who seemed to express interest in low-level programming of Android phones, no less, making him all the more suited to the task. La-Zu had found it a great waste of the kid's potential, having been locked in a mine for five years. Now he would serve the greater good, along with the rest of the subjects. All of them were strapped onto portable beds, set around the main I/O interface, high- latency fibre-optic cables wired into their implants. The last 24 hours had seen 76 percent of the encryption routine broken down. Which meant they only needed eight hours more.

A distant explosion could be heard, with gunfire following soon after. It sounded like the Allspace compound had been breached. La-Zu didn't see the need to worry then. The 418 had spared much expense in ensuring no one interfered with the decryption. Surely their men could handle it.

But when a series of explosions erupted near enough to shake the very foundations of the compound, La-Zu wasn't so sure. During his experiments, he had discovered the optimal perimeters to ensure that the minds of the DCs remained relaxed, and yet give an acceptable decryption bandwidth. This meant that the DCs were less likely to become brain-dead, and would require less frequent replacement. But now, time was of the essence. He could not have those ignorant attackers put a stop to this important operation, not when they were so close!

He would have to overclock the process by a magnitude of 16. These were the only DCs he had left, but there was no choice. The transfer of decrypted data would take but a few minutes. As La-Zu thumped the keyboard on the glowing interface, screams started emitting from the DCs. The 418 guards positioned around the Control Room cringed, but even non-intellectuals knew this had to be done. Despite the Dragon Head's orders to cease wireless communications except for field radios, La-Zu reopened a data transfer connection back to The Mountain's network server. Once decrypted, he had to transfer as much data as possible back to HQ.

The fate of the world depended on it. Lives could be replaced. Data could not.

This wasn't the movies, where a lone hero could take on the might of an entire army. This was real life, where every foe was almost as skilled as the hero was, where a stroke of misfortune could result in a stray bullet finding its way through a gap of the best NIJ-certified armour. Greg knew there was no way three men could fight against scores of similarly-armed and trained foes. But the many innovations of mankind included those meant for the military. And such innovations involved gaining an unfair advantage over each other.

The 418 storage area had a huge array of explosives, mainly anti-personnel weapons such as Claymores and fragmentation grenades. It also included less-than-lethal flashbangs, grenades intended to disorientate rather than kill, used when collateral damage is to be kept to a minimum. Greg would have gone for the lethal explosives alone, but there was too much at stake to risk collateral damage.

Loud bangs and flashes erupted throughout the room just like their namesakes. The large Control Room was lit up sporadically with a cacophony of noise and light, and there was nothing the 418 soldiers could do to stop it, eyes blinking hard as their hands clutched uselessly over their ears.

418 fell left and right without understanding why, the guns of the advancing intruders blazing decisively towards their skulls.

Greg yanked an earplug out with his free hand, as did his two companions. "Major Shang, cover that door!" he ordered. An electronic door stood closed at the far end of the room. Wesley had made a circuit around the room once before tapping away on a console set into the side of a large mainframe in the middle of the room. Four other rectangular structures were positioned around the wide space, but Greg couldn't see anything that would distinguish them from other subprocessor units. The floor here was of stainless steel grill, with pipes and wires visible beneath, indicator lights illuminating their snaking outlines.

The beds set around the central console like the dials of a clock caught his attention. Upon each and every one of them were children, their eyes glazed over as they shook as if from fits. Next to each of them was a display showing heart-rate, along with other variables that Greg didn't understand. One of the kids caught his attention.

"Jin!" yelled Greg, dashing over to the child lying on the side of the console opposite from the door. Finally up close to his son, Greg almost wept. Despite all his efforts, he never expected to come this far. The odds were stacked against him far too often: countless 418 guards, feral humans that wouldn't think twice about dismembering him for a meal, even a cult that could have zapped him with modified Super Soakers.

Greg held back a breath as his eyes drew over Jin. He was dressed in a plain white hospital gown, stained in places with the dark brown of dried blood. His face was much as Greg remembered it, only that his once gaunt cheeks were now more full, suggesting the 418 laboratories had fed him better. But what took Greg's breath away was the mess of wires connected to his head, an almost bizarre image seen only in science-fiction comics or movies.

The back and sides of his son's head were now a mess of connector ports, and Jin was jerking sporadically in his ... trance.

His brain was being wired to the server. Greg had to stop the connection. He reached a hand out towards the cables.

"Still your hand!" called Wesley, and Greg turned. The acolyte's eyes were stern. "Would you be instrumental to the death of a youngster?"

"The server's killing him!"

"Interrupting the process prematurely will result in descrambling of his brain. Just imagine the state of a corrupted hard drive."

"What can we do, then?" yelled Greg, stepping up towards the acolyte. "Can't you ... I don't know, shut down the process with that console, or something?"

"I already tried that. But the decryption progress is locked through an Administrator password, and it'll take too long to hack it manually," said Wesley. "However, I can access the root processes through my own neural stream, and try disconnecting the link between the subjects. I'll need you to cover me till then. With me connected to the brain network of the kids, a slight disturbance could prove dangerous." The acolyte reached at the back of his head, pulling forth a cable. "Can you do that, Greg?"

Greg knew that Wesley had come along for a reason. Not merely to save his son, or anyone else, for that matter. The data in the server meant more to the Brotherhood than anyone else. But he realised he had no choice.

"Do it fast." said Greg, and he dashed up to support Major Shang.

La-Zu shook in mingled anger and fear, peering from under the floor grille he was hiding beneath. All three interlopers wore the full battle armour of the Old Guard, yet they seemed to lack the characteristics of a fighting force. The one that seemed to be calling the shots appeared to recognise one of the DCs as his own. He and a near-emotionless soldier exchanged words—words that chilled La-Zu to the heart.

They were going to stop the decryption. After all his hard work, these ignorant fucks were going to put an end to all that! How could they understand that the fate of many outweighs the fate of a few useless kids? La-Zu was tempted to leap out of his hiding space, and do whatever it took to defend his brainchild. Not that it would mean much, and the two guards would easily cut him down where he stood.

One of the 418 soldiers had fallen right next to edge of the grille opening. La-Zu's eyes picked up the M110 Sniper rifle hanging over the edge. Equipped with both long range scope along with iron-sights for close combat, La-Zu knew the semi-automatic weapon was loaded with 7.62mm armour-piercing rounds. More than enough to deal with these armoured thugs. Getting up slowly from where he sat, La-Zu prised the weapon strap away from the dead guard, ignoring the clatter of the gun over the railing. He would have to take care of the two guards first. Having been connected to the console, the third won't be able to respond.

These ignorants would pay.

■

"Did you hear that?" asked Major Shang suddenly, his eyes sweeping the room. Greg thought he had heard a clattering, but with the slight hum that dominated the whole place, he had dismissed it as background noise.

He caught a quick movement out of the corner of his eye. Trying to throw himself to the side, Greg instead stumbled against the cover he had braced against instead. Even as he tried to bring up his oh-so-heavy SAW, he knew he would never be able to fire first.

Major Shang moved faster than Greg could imagine, darting before him. The roar of several shots rang out, and Greg felt the Major fall back onto him, bringing him down in a heap.

La-Zu turned his gun on Wesley, just as Greg brought his own up. Two shots rang out as one.

Wesley yelled, and all at once, the children in the circle shuddered together with him. Heart rate sensors beeped, and several of them meandered out into a flat line. Greg's target fell backward with a gurgle, his rifle falling with a clatter on the ground. An alarm sounded in the far distance, and Greg then knew somehow, the condition of the server's subjects was linked to the call for reinforcements. Yells sounded in the sealed door beyond.

"Leave me! I'll be fine!" Wesley said through gritted teeth. He pulled out another syrette of neurostimulant, jabbing the needle into his neck. Greg checked on the kids. A few appear to have died, presumably because of the neural dump Wesley's injury gave them. But Jin appeared to be fine, if only for his heart rate becoming far more erratic. The disengagement percentage progress on the screen seemed to increase faster, and Greg knew that with several kids dead, less minds would have to be entangled from their mental slavery. Which meant that if he were to shoot several more kids, Jin had a good chance …

A choking noise caught his attention, and Greg turned his attention towards it. Here, Major Shang lay dying, while he contemplated murder most foul? These kids belonged to other parents just like him. He rushed towards his compatriot, who now slumped against one of the processor units. As Greg knelt beside him, drawing a first aid dressing, he already knew the injury was far more than he could handle. From the amount of blood pooling out from the front of the Major's chest where his armour plate was, he didn't have long. As Greg tried to remove the Major's vest, he grasped Greg's hand and pulled him close.

"After you save the kids ... take good care of Guo Li ..." He choked.

"I will, Major," assured Greg, fighting hard against the Major's grip. "Just let me wrap up your wound ..."

The Major's grip tightened so hard that Greg gasped. "Promise me!"

Greg didn't know how things would be like after all this was over. Will it be truly over, for that matter? After he had saved his son, and Wesley got what he came for, the 418 would be after them all. Not even the Old Guard could stand against their might. But Major Shang and his men had risked all they had to help him, and it would be remiss to turn away from what they stood for: protection of the innocent.

If he could take care of two kids before, he could do it again.

"I promise." With that, Major Shang smiled, and closed his eyes.

The door to the server room groaned open, mechanical motors straining against underused roller bearings. Through the gap in the door that had formed, a familiar war chant of the 418 could be heard.

The Dragon snakes his coils around,
The Phoenix dances forth!
The Dragon chases the Pearl around,
The Phoenix is reborn!
With a breath almighty cold,
Like the Dragon we purge our foes!
Dragon Head! Dragon Head!
We fight in your name!
To purify, to conquer,
To absolve of shame …

Greg shouldered the sling of his SAW, a sense of calm emanating through him. He should be exhausted, having spent much of the night awake and without rest. But all things considered, what he was about to face was nothing compared to what he had braved so far. When this was over, there was so much he could teach Jin. And Guo Li too.

He just had to survive a little longer. Greg ducked behind one of the processors facing the steadily-opening door, and fired upon the advancing enemy.

The Code was the Law, and the Law was To Exist.

For years, Wesley had partaken in the sermons the Administrator gave his flock. Though it emphasised belief in the intangible rather than physical, Wesley always kept a foot in both worlds. After all, how could the Code exist without a physical vessel to broadcast itself? Even after the Implants of Transcending Reception had been installed within his cranium, Wesley was not without belief that the physical world held as much value as the digital. Which is why he understood Greg's need to recover his son.

It was no easy task trying to untangle the security protocols associated with each kid. Intentional or not, every mind connected to the digital realm exhibited some degree of resistance when one attempted to access it. Coupled with the fact that these kids had been beaten and tortured by their captors. This subconscious fear increases one's resistance to intrusion, and Wesley was sure that the 418 scientists must have known that, if only by accident.

Being fired upon disrupted his concentration, but the connection Wesley had established in the minds of the children caused them to share his intense pain. A number of them died from the shock outright, while the rest screamed and writhed. The feeling of despair and unfairness their neural dumps routed threatened to disengage his own cortex processors, and it was all Wesley could do to inject a neurorelaxant into himself, and apply pressure to his wound. He needed his entire concentration if this was to work.

Not that he wasn't aware of what went on around him. He could see and hear Greg composing himself as he made one last promise to Major Shang, not just from where he stood, but from multiple angles. Wesley could see the 418 soldiers massed outside a huge door in great detail, complete with their tattoos and equipment, and it was then that he realised he had gotten access to the compound's intranet. Through that, he got access to the security cameras, though the total number of visible feeds were incomplete.

The children were not just decryption proxies. They also had the network key installed inside them. And when a few of them died, parts of the data making up the key had been transferred to all of them, including him. Which meant that he now had partial access to the server, but not yet that of Network Administrator.

Wesley knew he could use a worm to pry the network key off the children, but that would result in neural breakdown, giving rise to brain death. Although he was sure the other members of his brotherhood would not hesitate, the fact that he had known a kid in person would make it a personal betrayal if he did.

Steeling his mind, he knew he had another, less pleasant choice. The sharing of minds was done during the daily communion back in the Sanctum, where the members of the Brotherhood put their minds together via wired connection to a server chatroom. The theory behind it was to ensure everyone could motivate each other towards a common goal. It may work, given time, but the fact that everyone had their own wants, desires and hates so different from his made it a rather uncomfortable process. And now he had to do it with kids. Wesley barely remembered his childhood, but he did remember how boisterous and full of life children were whenever his relatives came over during major holidays before The Storm. They were always talking twenty to the dozen, clambering over his furniture, and messing with his computer's wired connections and encryption devices his workplace let him use. It had cost him years of building the perfect workstation.

No time like the present. Wesley steeled himself as he opened a firewall to the children, fragmented thoughts washing over him. Hopefully, these strangers would be more helpful than his relatives' brats ever were.

Greg gritted his teeth as he fell back behind cover, a long trail of blood running down his arm. The 418 soldiers coming through the door were relentless, and for several he put down, more took their place. A wild shot had gone through his unprotected arm, and it was all Greg could do not to falter in his defence. Several 418 troopers had even rushed in with ballistic shields, but two of the Major's grenades had made short work of them, leaving them writhing and screaming on the floor. Sometime in the last three minutes, the electronic door had started closing. Only a few of the 418 soldiers had made it inside before it shut completely, but Greg knew his position was precarious. The 418 soldiers had dug in behind cover, and flushing them out would be far too risky, especially with his injury. Already some of them laid covering fire upon him, their loud echoes bouncing off the magnetically-shielded walls. Right across Greg was Major Shang, his lifeless eyes staring back at Greg.

No more foes could enter the server room, but for all it mattered, the place was already gone. He alone couldn't take on the few 418 that made it inside, especially when he was down to about 15 rounds of ammo, according to his translucent magazine. He had the Major's P228 pistol, but that wouldn't be of much use even against light body armour. Wesley shook erratically, the protocols of the server fast taking a toll on his mind. Meanwhile, one of the 418 soldiers had gained ground, peering around at Wesley.

Greg couldn't risk him getting shot. Not with his son in there, not with Wesley still alive. "Get down, Wesley!" he yelled, yanking his last grenade out from a pouch.

The digital world has a different perception of time. With the extremely high speed of processing, every hour spent inside it could feel like an entire year, or two. Which goes to say that the last few minutes inside felt like weeks.

There were a lot of things one could do with so much time and bandwidth. With several enthusiastic kids helping out, that speed is multiplied. Picobytes upon picobytes of data that would take the fastest computers hours to process took only the space of minutes.

Wesley knew he may not survive, but he had done all he can.

The wall to the control room exploded, taking Greg by surprise. Everything was thrown about by the force of the shockwave—corpses, fighters, cultist and 418 alike. Greg coughed and made to open his eyes, but the haze of dust caused him to blink in futility. His ballistic goggles had come loose in the chaos.

Dark figures swept into the room, the room's lighting flashing sporadically. The emergency lighting flicked on, illuminating the room with a red glow, giving the newcomers an almost supernatural appearance. As Greg made to get up, one of the figures shoved him back down with a boot, pinning him to the debris-lined floor. The barrel of a battle rifle pressed against his neck, stilling whatever resistance he had remaining. His head already turned to the right, Greg could only watch on as several of the figures kicked a motionless Wesley. In the brief flickers of the main lighting, Greg could see that the newcomers were decked out in what had to be the best armour and weapons in the wasteland. What looked to be black ceramic scales outlined in red covered their forms from head to toe, and

Greg was willing to bet few weapons in the wasteland could hope to pierce it. In their hands were an assortment of Belgian-made SCAR-Hs, which Greg knew had to be pilfered from a commando camp or that of an elite police unit. The 418 soldiers that managed to make it into the control room earlier knelt before them.

"We give our respects to the Dragon Head and Teeth!" announced one of the soldiers, a senior 49er, if Greg could guess from his scarred appearance.

"Your orders were to capture the control room," spoke a voice among the scaled figures. "You have however failed. Only the strong survive."

"Only the strong survive!" intoned the scaled troopers. The control room was lit up by the harsh staccato of gunfire. The 418 failures fell to the ground, and Greg did all he could not to gasp. This guy just ordered his own men killed. He only had to imagine how he would treat his enemies.

Out of the group stepped a figure. He wore robes of the blackest silk, with numerous red dragon motifs interspersed throughout it. He grew out a beard that would have been long out of fashion before The Storm, and eyes that were crueller than anyone Greg had seen. Before he even spoke, Greg knew this had to be the leader of the 418. How could it not be? No one else would be escorted by fighters with equipment that would eclipse even a modern pre-Storm army. A bodyguard pulled Greg's helmet off, and the Dragon Head snapped his fingers.

A man was brought before them, hands bound behind him. Though his hair was now dishevelled, and his skin stained with grime and layers upon layers of dried blood, Greg recognised him still.

It was Lantern, his nighttime guide through the labs of the 418.

"Do you recognise this man, Lantern?" asked the Dragon Head almost lazily. He had taken to twirling his pistol around his index finger. It wasn't a model Greg recognised. Custom-made too, if the reflex sight and red matt finish was any indication.

"Yes, Dragon Ho," coughed Lantern. Greg stared defiantly back at him.

"Look carefully. I'd really hate to kill the wrong guy," droned Dragon Ho. "Is he or is he not?"

Lantern's eyes bored into Greg's face, such that he was tempted to damn it all and make one last fight for it.

"I'm positive, Dragon Ho. This is the one that infiltrated The Mountain, and forced me to take him to the labs."

"That'll be all." Dragon Ho raised his pistol and fired.

Lantern collapsed with barely a sound, not even a gurgle. The bodyguards caught hold of him, throwing him beside Greg. Greg thought his time had come, but still Dragon Ho toyed with him. The 418 leader stepped before him, looking disdainfully at his prone self.

"There are many things you can tell about someone through their eyes," said Dragon Ho. "The lies they keep, the anger they harbour. Even their penchant for vengeance. I see all of that in you.

You were most resourceful too, if your exploits are to be believed, but I have but one question. What made you do all of this? Self-righteousness? The wish to upsurp my rule? I didn't think so."

Greg would have contended with a "fuck you", but he wasn't ready to die just yet. "You took my son away. I've come to get him back."

"So that's what it was." Dragon Ho nodded. "A quest of retrieval, much like the stories of old. But at great risk you put your life to find him. It could have resulted in you lying dead on a highway, alone and forgotten. It could have resulted in you being a victim of the barbarians that roam the highways. Your son might not even have been alive anymore, for that matter. Did you think that you, a mere slave miner, could hope to face off against the 418 empire and win? All that you had done was for naught." With that, Dragon Ho fired at the children lying around the console. Each and every one of them jerked from the force of the shot, heads slumping to their sides.

"No!" yelled Greg. He made to move, but one of the bodyguards held him down. He would have thrown him off and charged Dragon Ho, but this guy was far too strong. It was like trying to move a tank. Despair seeped into him as he realised he would never talk to Jin again, never get to hold him as he went to sleep.

"What you feel is but a fraction of the pain you have caused me," hissed Dragon Ho. "All we had been working towards, to rebuild a new world, set back by the stupidity of just one individual! Don't you understand? Your son means nothing! People mean nothing! Without the knowledge of the world before, what does it matter if people live like rats in a hole? All my people are doing is change all that for the better, and yet your ignorance set us back by a margin of a few years! But no matter, once the Old Guard are finished, there won't be anyone to stand against us."

When I shout, run towards the door, said a voice in Greg's head.

What? thought Greg, wondering if he had imagined it. Dragon Ho levered his pistol at Greg's head, and Greg could hardly make out his words in his fear.

"I will live in The Cloud!" yelled a voice, and everyone's heads jerked towards Wesley. The acolyte had both his hands clutched around what had to be a telescopic antenna, and Greg immediately knew who had spoken in his mind. Summoning the last of his strength, he sprung upright, shoving his armoured guard before him.

Explosions rang out in the room beyond where they stood, followed by an enormous one from Wesley, engulfing everything around in a ball of fire. Greg felt himself sliding backwards with the guard he held against him as a shield, his back slamming hard against a wall. His back hurt, his body hurt, but he remembered what he had been told. The emergency lights of the room flickered on and off, and the sound of rushing water could be heard.

The whole place was starting to flood, no doubt from a burst pipe. Already he could hear splashes of water where Dragon's Teeth bodyguards staggered from the aftereffects of the blast. Shoving his scorched, smoking guard to the ground, Greg dashed towards the electronic door to the room, which appeared to have been partially blown open. 418 soldiers that had been waiting to enter lay in the hallway beyond, stunned or mangled by the explosive charges. He chanced a glance at where Wesley was, and with great regret, saw only a blast mark and what remained of his gear.

The acolyte had sacrificed himself.

Several shots rang out behind Greg, and one of them hit him on the torso. He yelled, forcing himself to keep running even as he felt an intense pain beneath his rear armour plate. Out in the hallway, pandemonium greeted him. 418 soldiers ran left and right, trying to find the nearest way out. The water flooding the compound was now at knee level, making it hard to run. The poor lighting didn't help matters, throwing shadows all over the place, confusing pipes and fixtures with doorways and entrances.

There's a lift at the end of the hallway, said the voice in his head. *Go to it.*

"Wesley?" gasped Greg aloud. "I saw you die!"

Death is but a new beginning, said the voice. *Go now, and hurry. The armoured thugs are after you.*

Greg wondered how this being, whoever he was, knew. But several security cameras in the area gave him cause to believe that was how. As he waded his way forward, the wound on his side making it nearly impossible, a door opened 10 metres away. Greg recognised the interior as that of a lift, and forced himself to move faster.

He managed to clamber inside, and despite the flooding, the buttons of the lift were still lit.

Pressing G, the highest floor he could go, Greg struck the Close button.

A hand found itself in between the doors, preventing the lift door from closing. It was Dragon Ho. Surprisingly agile despite his age, Greg should have forseen that the 418 leader, not being bogged down by the cumbersome armour of his bodyguards, was able to catch up with him. The 418 leader's face was a mess of scars, the entire left of which was burned, giving him an almost maniacal appearance. His robe was shredded in places, but the lack of blood suggested it had given him some bodily protection. Integrated ballistic fabric, no doubt.

"Not so fast, cheebai kia!" yelled Dragon Ho, ruler of the 418. He clambered into the lift and swung a slim blade towards Greg, missing in his disorientation. He must have lost his gun in Wesley's last stand.

So close to safety, Greg had had enough of this shit. Whipping out the P228 pistol he had gotten from Major Shang, he fired not once, but five times at Dragon Ho's unprotected face. As the scumbag crumpled against the doorway, Greg pressed the Close button once more.

The water was now at chest level, and steadily rising, and Greg worried for a moment that the weight of the water would ground the lift entirely. But the designers must have accounted for such an eventuality, because the lift rose, then flooded completely.

His entire self surrounded by water, Greg held his breath, straining to hold it all in. The occasional explosion in the compound below pounded through his ears, and he wondered just how long would it take for the goddamn lift to reach the bloody top already. Then he realised that with the compound being a high-security one, it probably ran quite deep underground, much like CERN, the European research facility. He then realised that for all his and Wesley's efforts, he was going to drown in this metal coffin, and no one would ever know.

The lift shuddered to a stop, and Greg's eyes glazed over, knowing his time had come. Then the door opened, sending him and hundreds of litres of water flooding out onto oh-so-solid land. His face to the ground, Greg gasped in deep breaths as shadows loomed over him. At this point of time, he didn't care if the 418 strung him up, as long as he had air to breathe.

"I sure didn't expect anyone to make it out of there," commented one of the newcomers. "Least of all in a flooded lift."

"Cease your talk, ITm4ster, and see to the crusader," snapped a voice all too familiar to Greg. "Let not Wesley's efforts be in vain."

EPILOGUE

Greg was an honoured resident of the Sanctum, The Utopia and The City. He held the honorary titles of Mediator and Peacekeeper, serving as a bridge between the common people and their leaders. Though he spent the first three years in The City in order to raise Guo Li, he regularly travelled among the different settlements and helped where he could. Often it was water and land disputes, but occasionally, there were external threats that had to be addressed. Bandit gangs new and old still posed a problem, along with rogue pockets of 418 loyalists.

Guo Li's upbringing had been mostly taken care of by the late Major Shang. His fierce desire to serve the community meant that it was all Greg could do to prevent him from being overzealous. Out of necessity, children grew up quickly in the wasteland. By the time he was 14, he was going on perimeter duty with the rest of the men, even participating in two of the raids on bandits holed up in the old Haw Par Villa theme park and the PSA Vista building. Guo Li thus became a valued soldier among the ranks of the Old Guard, and despite wishing to keep him safe, Greg knew he wouldn't have been happy anywhere else.

The BOC were also in the process of modifying surviving smartphones and tablets to receive satellite signals. So far, only key personnel in the communities such as Greg had them and they were used mainly for status updates and emergency communications. Greg received a message one day while he was inspecting the outdoor sanitation at Marina New Town. People had been using the nearby Singapore River as both a source of water and dumping area for their waste, and Greg was discussing plans with the community leaders to limit unnecessary access to the river.

"Hang on," Greg said to the foreman. He took out his RugGear phone and thumbed the screen on. A white envelope showed at the top of his screen. Rather surprised, as none of the communities had SMS functionality yet, Greg opened the message.

<Call me.> was all it said. The sender's number was listed as <OVERSEAS * ERROR* >.

Greg's finger hovered over the green Call button. He had experienced enough crap in his lifetime to know that it was always a bad idea to return a call to an unknown caller. There were enough phone scams from before The Storm, and they may have experienced a resurgence the moment some semblance of technology returned to the world.

Another message popped up. <Not a scam, Greg.>

So this person knew his name. Even if it was a disgruntled 418 soldier bent on giving him an expletive-filled threat, he could get this over and done with. Pressing the Call Back button, Greg braced himself and listened. There wasn't a dial tone, given that the signal wasn't transmitted by a standard phone network, so Greg wondered if he was doing it right.

It's so peaceful here.

Greg dropped the phone, cursing as he did. The foreman and his assistants looked back at Greg, and the Peacekeeper waved to show it was nothing. He gingerly picked up the phone. Still working, though, so Greg placed it against his ear.

Your face was a riot, you know that? came the amused voice from before.

"Wesley?" gasped Greg. For years, he had believed the acolyte had passed on, never to speak again. "What's going on? How can you see me? Where are you?"

So quick to ask. So many questions, laughed the voice. *As always, I have been in The Cloud. You will forgive me if I didn't speak to you earlier, but until my old fraternity had restored the more mundane means of human communication, I had no way of getting in touch with you. Besides, I have been busy.*

Greg wondered what anyone could possibly be busy with if they had gone over to the other side. But then, Wesley was as hardworking in death as in life, as his exploits following the incident with the server had shown.

If you were wondering how I could see your impression of a comedian, it was through the selfie camera on your brick of a phone, continued Wesley.

Greg snorted. "RugGear phones were built to last. But enough about me. How are you doing there?" Greg gave a pause. "And how's Jin?"

Jin has been left to his own devices. In The Cloud, we of the Flesh-Free are able to go where we please, explained Wesley. *We are neither master nor slave. You have to let your son go, Greg, or such wishes will consume you. I believe Guo Li is well? The communications logs say that much.*

"You can access our signals?" asked Greg. That didn't sound secure.

Each and every member of the Brotherhood has a unique network footprint. Given that I am something of a divinity, the Administrator himself allowed me full access. This way, I can make improvements regarding latency and connection issues.

"Can't have the internet hanging when someone accesses a webpage, right?" Greg said. He could, however, hear the hint of a sigh in Wesley's voice. "Is there anything wrong, Wesley?"

There was a pause so long, that Greg thought Wesley had disconnected. When he next spoke, it was wistful and weary, as if he had travelled a long way.

In my time in The Cloud, I have seen and learnt so many things. I have travelled through network directories to data stores displaying information I had never envisaged the human race to be capable of creating even fifty years from now. But in one directory exists a link to a file that could mean the difference between life and death on Earth. That file is not in the interconnected satellite network, and appears to have been moved some time after The Storm happened. And the network signature responsible for that has not been created by any computer program written by man.

"So … what exactly are you saying?" Greg asked.

Someone had set the file to move itself when a catastrophe of unprecedented scale occurs. Each and every device, be it a laptop or smartphone, leaves a unique network signature that can be traced back to its origin. The fact that this wasn't created by a human computer suggests these are beings we don't know of. They moved a very rare and important file that defined the human race in its extremities. If that file remains lost, who's to say what could happen when another Storm claims everyone? There'll be no one left to do anything about it.

"Wesley, what is on that file?" asked Greg quietly. The transcended acolyte's voice was deathly serious, and Greg knew this to be no laughing matter.

The file is gone, but the contents description that remains in the link directory indicates it shows the Past, Present and Future. Greg, when I accessed the directory, it set off an alert to multiple recipients, to whom, I don't know. But they aren't of this world. There're going to be others on the trail of this file, and you cannot allow them to have it!

Greg felt a deep trepidation rising within him. Around him, people went about their normal lives, believing they would be forever safe from those who would take their freedom from them. Parents were showing their children how to set up water catchment devices before the sun set, and a carpenter and his apprentice were building a seesaw for the community playground. And now Wesley was telling him all this was for naught.

"Wesley, who are after the file?" asked Greg. "If not people, then who?"

Beings not of this world. Aliens. Wesley's voice sounded frantic.

"Wesley, let's be logical here. You and I know that aliens don't exist." Greg's voice now had an edge to it.

No one believed The Storm would ever happen, but it did, argued Wesley. *Is it really so difficult to believe? Out of the billions upon billions of galaxies, not to mention planets, what are the chances that Earth is the only one capable of sustaining life? Has it occurred to you that there are beings much greater and superior in technology, who have been observing us from the very start? They might even have caused The Storm. Greg, if the world is to come to an end again, don't you want to know when it may happen? It's not just a duty to yourself, the Old Guard, the Brotherhood, or even the community at large. The human race depends on it. You have to find the file before those who wish the human race harm gets hold of it—*

Wesley's voice died in a crackle of static so loud that Greg yelled, almost dropping his phone as he drew it away. He forced himself to listen, and thought he could hear garbled screams in the static. And then a disembodied voice came, a voice with an intonation that was a mix of animal and machine, and could not have been vocalised by a human throat.

Your time will come.

Greg's phone indicated a new message, and he quickly opened it. Upon it a series of numbers and parentheses, a pattern that Greg recognised as longitude and latitude. That was where the file might be. That was where he had to find the last remnant that gave a clue to how the Future might be shaped. He had to summon the Commander of the Old Guard and the Administrator, where they might discuss a plan of action, and perhaps even contribute men to a task bigger than any of his previous undertakings. They may even have to get the help of the ex-navy personnel and skilled labour to build a boat that would be able to take him to these coordinates. Perhaps even an entire fleet to bring several specialist teams with him.

But one thing Greg knew for sure. The future had never looked so bleak, and The Storm was merely the beginning.

ACKNOWLEDGEMENTS

The Last Server was birthed forth from an idea I had in 2013, and it is with much joy that I'm finally been able to see it in print. Just like Greg's journey across post-apocalyptic Singapore, not every journey is completed alone. I would thus like to take the opportunity to thank the follow individuals who helped make this book possible.

Chris Mooney-Singh and Savinder Singh, who organised the Mentor Access Programme, during which I completed the manuscript. Without the MAP, I might never have completed the first draft of the novel.

Desmond Kon, who mentored me during the entirety of the MAP. His suggestions and analysis of my draft helped me consider the best way to introduce events in the novel.

The Arts House for sending my work for editorial feedback at Textures 2019.

Anita Teo and She-reen Wong of Marshall Cavendish who gave me the chance of having my first novel published.

My friend, Ellery, who accompanied me on my field trip around Marina Bay to research possible location scenes in *The Last Server*, let me bounce story ideas off him and helped read through the first draft.

My cousin Kheng Wee who gave feedback on the first draft.

National Arts Council, who allowed me and the other mentees of MAP the opportunity to give a book reading in SWF 2016, and to be a featured author at SWF 2019.

My mother who first introduced me to the Singapore Writer's Festival. She also backed me by means of never discouraging and reminding me my writing wasn't a complete waste of time.

Last but not least, to all you dear readers, who are willing to accompany Greg and I on this journey.

ABOUT THE AUTHOR

H.J. Pang has been writing since 2007. After proving his worth for two years in the Singapore army, H.J. got a degree in mechanical design and spent some time as a design engineer. He is currently working on his Master's thesis involving thermal damage in carbon fibre. While not doing experiments and writing research papers, H.J. is traipsing around the country, writing whenever he can while travelling in one of two forms of public transportation.